AR 4 6
6 pts

AUG 1 3 2014

W9-AUC-343

What
Every Girl
(except me)
Knows

What Every Girl (except me) Knows

A Novel by

NORA RALEIGH BASKIN

Little, Brown and Company
Boston New York London

First Edition

The characters and events portrayed in this book are fictitious. Any similarity to real persons, living or dead, is coincidental and not intended by the author.

Library of Congress Cataloging-in-Publication Data

Baskin, Nora Raleigh.
    What every girl (except me) knows / by Nora Raleigh Baskin. — 1st ed.
    p. cm.
    Summary: Twelve-year-old Gabby feels that she needs a mother to help her grow into a woman, so when things between her father and his latest girlfriend do not work out, Gabby sets off for the last place she remembers seeing her own mother.
    ISBN 0-316-07021-1
    [1. Identity — Fiction. 2. Mothers — Fiction. 3. Friendship — Fiction.
4. Death — Fiction.] I. Title.

PZ7.B29233 Wh 2001
[Fic] — dc21   00-040557

10 9 8 7 6 5 4 3 2 1

MV-NY

Printed in the United States of America

The text was set in Joanna and Clyde, and the display type is Dado.

$\mathcal{A}$s I become one in a long line of grateful writers, I give my truest thanks to friend and novelist Elinor Lipman for simply making my dream come true.

Thank you to Maria Modugno of Little, Brown, who from the first minute she spoke to me did so with generosity and warmth, and whose skill and insight I quickly learned to trust.

To Robin Rue of Writers House, for wise counsel and a kind voice; thank you for both.

To Erin Anderson and Kristin Millay, my young, first readers, who dropped everything and read, whenever I asked them to.

To my dad, Hank Raleigh, and my brother, Stephen Raleigh, with so much love.

And to all my YBFs, who keep me going.

Love and thanks to my husband, Steve, and my boys, Sam and Ben, without whom none of this would mean much at all.

For my mother

Part I

Chapter 1

My Journal

I've been keeping a journal now for almost a full year. Actually, I have three journals. One is for dreams, one is for important stuff like this, and one is a list. My list journal is called "Things I Need to Know to Be a Woman."

First I wrote in "woman." Then I crossed that out and wrote in "girl." Then I crossed that out and wrote in "woman" again. I still can't decide.

I'm assuming I'll turn into a woman someday whether I know anything about being one or not. I think Amber Whitman already has, because every month she goes to the nurse with a mysterious stomachache. We learned all about that in health, and everyone saw the movie. So Amber's not fooling anyone.

But being like a girl (or womanly or girlish or feminine, whatever you want to call it) is something you definitely have to learn.

Girls probably don't even know they're learning it. It just gets absorbed into them while they are sleeping. But one thing for certain is that it has to come from a mother.

And a mother is one thing I don't have. Not since I was three years old, too long ago to miss her. Too long ago to even remember her. So I keep a list.

My dad's girlfriend two years ago came over once to make veal scallopini. She took this skinny meat, dipped it in egg, and then into flour, and then into bread crumbs. Then she cooked it on the stove. I wrote that all down on my list.

Another one of my dad's girlfriends used a comb to tease up her hair and make it look fuller. She actually lifted her hair on top of her head, held it up in the air, and sort of combed it backward. I saw her in the bathroom when the door fell open a little. She got mad when she looked in the mirror and saw me behind her, watching.

"A little privacy, sweetie, please," she said.

And she knocked the door shut with her foot, because her hands were too busy with a comb and a big wad of tangled hair. She only came over that once, though, and I already had the information for my list.

But watching Cleo Bloom is better than it's been with anyone else. Cleo is into this "open" thing. My dad hasn't dated anyone else but Cleo for almost a year now.

Cleo caught me watching her, and she didn't even

say anything. She was standing in the kitchen rubbing hand cream into her hands. First she squirted a little bit from the bottle onto the backs of her hands. Then she massaged it all around, into her fingers, even her fingernails, and then up her arms to her elbows. When she saw me staring she just laughed.

"Old elbows," she told me. "A woman's elbows always give her age away."

Then she held the bottle out to me.

I shook my head. I had known Cleo for all these months but I had never hung out with her before. I wasn't used to her yet. Usually she and my dad went out and I stayed home with my brother, Ian. Lately, though, she is around a lot more.

I just checked out my elbows in the full-length mirror inside my closet door. My elbows are different from Cleo's. Cleo's are more wrinkly, like there is extra skin puckering out. She isn't so old, though. I think maybe thirty-three or something. My dad is forty-two.

My elbows still look young, I guess. I'm only twelve.

Chapter 2

"She's coming and she'll cry." Lynette leaned over her desk till she was practically dropping out of her seat. She had already said the same crazy thing three times.

Lynette was strange and extremely unpopular, which probably was the reason she was making such an effort to talk to me. Since I, of late, had been nice to her. The truth is, I felt sorry for her ever since this little fourth grader on my bus told me that Lynette had been hit by a truck when she was a baby in her stroller. Nobody was supposed to know that, but this little kid heard it from her cousin or something, and she told everyone. She told me last week, on the way home from school. The sun was already low, trapped behind the Catskill Mountains, leaving us a cold, gray ride home.

"My cousin said the girl was hit by a truck when she was in her stroller. Were you ever hit by a truck?" she asked, I presumed me, since we were the last two riders on the bus.

"Why, do I look like it?" I said, looking out the window at the river. Our bus followed the same meandering path as the Wallkill River. At points the river ribboned close to the road and was visible. I liked to see the river slipping by, as quiet as the trees standing on its muddy banks; quieter still than the secrets I imagined were carried with it.

"No, you don't look like you've been hit by a truck. I just didn't know you could be hit by a truck and live. But this girl's in the same grade as you. I thought you would know her."

"So who is it?" I asked, finally.

"I shouldn't tell." She lifted up her chin. "It wouldn't be nice. If you can't say something nice, don't say anything at all."

There. That was one of those things. Girls are supposed to say nice things. They compliment each other on their outfits and their haircuts. They offer to do things without being asked, like bring homemade cookies to a party or clear the dishes after supper. Even when they're mean, girls are nice about it.

"Well, telling me someone's name would be a very nice thing to say," I said, not thinking it would really work, not caring in the first place.

"Lynette," the kid blurted out.

I guess she hadn't had enough "girl" stuff absorbed into her yet.

She had meant Lynette Waters, who was right at the moment desperately trying to talk to me.

"She's coming and she'll cry," Lynette said for the fourth time.

"All right already, who's coming?" I turned to face Lynette.

"A new girl in sixth grade. I heard it in the office," Lynette told me.

Lynette and I had had the same homeroom assignment for the last two years. Waters and Weiss. And weren't we lucky, because the last name of the most popular girl in sixth grade was Whitman. Amber Whitman. Somehow, we all ended up in last-period math class together, too.

"The new girl is going to be in our homeroom," Lynette said a little too loudly.

"A new girl?" Amber turned around in her seat. Her hair moved with her like a blond waterfall. "What's her name?"

Lynette thought a moment, as if trying to remember. "I don't know her name," Lynette said, worried.

Our math teacher was explaining how to change decimals into fractions when she suddenly stopped and looked up from her book.

"Not likely," Amber whispered, and she immediately flipped back around in her chair.

"She's coming and she'll cry," Lynette said quietly to me when the teacher was turned and again writing on the board. "And I am thinking who she is."

I was thinking, too. I could use a new friend. Amber Whitman had her popular friends — the ones who ate lunch every day at the same table headed by none other than Amber herself. They performed gymnastic moves on the playground each day and held secret meetings in the bathroom to rate the other kids in school.

Even Lynette had her two best friends, both of them kind of weird, too, but they constituted a group.

No one liked Rhonda Littleman, the smartest girl in the whole sixth grade, but she happily made up her own group of one, sometimes two if you included boys, because Alex Bassik was so smart that no one else talked to him.

Then there was the group of tough girls who had homemade tattoos and who smoked cigarettes behind the bleachers before school. Patty Parker had her boyfriend's name poked into her wrist with india ink and a needle. Carl. But it came out looking like *Larl* because, she said, she messed up on the C.

But I was miserably free. (I had never had a real, real best friend. And I couldn't count Mimi Russo just because she was in after-school day care with me every day from kindergarten till fourth grade. Anyway, her dad got relocated and she moved two years ago.) I moved around from group to group, friend to friend. So even though I prided myself with not being stuck on any one peg, I wondered — *Who will the new girl be?*

I was daydreaming like that when the bell rang and someone slapped me on the back.

"Let's go, Gabby. You're going to miss the bus." It was Peter Scalzi.

He headed out to the lockers, and I got up and followed. Peter was kind of short. He had buzzed hair and a funny face, but he was a really good athlete and that put him in with the popular boys, automatically. He had been in my class every year since kindergarten, except third and fifth. He was still in a lot of my classes this year, even though this was the first year we switched around from subject to subject.

One of the dreams that I have recorded in my dream journal over and over is that I miss my bus home. I dream that I am standing at my locker and I can't get it open. My legs feel like they are twisted in rubber, and I have to struggle to get to the bus line, and when I get there I can't find which bus is mine. In some dreams, I see my bus but it's too late. It leaves without me.

Last week, I mistakenly confided in Rhonda Littleman about my dream journal, because she had just done an oral report called "The Mysteries of the Mind." I told her about my recurring bus nightmare.

She said that something was wrong with me, because most people dreamt about missing their ride to school or to work — it represented anxiety. Dreaming about missing the bus home was pathologic.

Like I said — telling Rhonda was a mistake. What did she know, anyway? I think I hated her.

I grabbed my coat out of my locker, and with my backpack banging against my legs I ran for the bus. I prayed, between huffing and puffing, I wasn't going to miss it. No one would be home to pick me up if I did. My dad had student critiques at the college Wednesday afternoons.

"Wait!" I knocked on the tall doors. The bus driver looked down three steps at me. I waved up at him, pathetically.

"Almost didn't make it," Mr. Worthington told me as he maneuvered the doors to open.

"Almost," I said, stepping inside.

Then I wished I hadn't. Debbie Curtis sat in the only available seat not filled with three people. I really was afraid of Debbie Curtis. I had heard that her father was a prison guard at the Wallkill State Penitentiary. Her brothers were both football players at the high school. Sizewise, the family resemblance was unmistakable.

I had no choice. I sat down and right on cue Debbie Curtis hissed, "You look so stupid."

I saw someone on the *Oprah Winfrey Show* once who said to respond with "So?" to anything a bully says. But it didn't seem like that was going to help. I thought it best to remain silent in this situation.

Debbie decided to explain her uninvited commentary. "You look like a *boy* in that old coat."

Now, I knew that my coat was not old. It was new, actually. It was a dark-olive, drab, down bubble jacket. My brother had one just like it. But now in addition to looking like I was ready to go two hundred miles behind a dogsled team, it seemed I looked like a boy.

"You'd look like a boy if you were wearing a *prom* dress," I said and braced myself, my fingers clutching the edge of the seat.

Debbie Curtis gave me one big shove, and despite my

grip I landed in the rubber aisle between the seats. I could see Mr. Worthington's frowning eyes in the rearview mirror.

"Sit down behind me," he said. There was always one bench seat directly behind the driver, reserved for trouble-makers, and no one could sit there unless ordered to. I think Mr. Worthington knew he was doing me a favor. I gladly moved up and slipped behind his seat. I looked up to thank him, but Mr. Worthington's eyes were now fixed on the road.

Rhonda Littleman was wrong about one more thing — riding home on the bus *did* represent anxiety.

Chapter 3

When I got home from school, Cleo was in the kitchen chopping up raw vegetables. I wasn't so surprised to see real vegetables instead of the frozen ones we usually had, but I was surprised to see Cleo at my house in the middle of the week; surprised to see Cleo at my house when my dad wasn't home.

I did quickly take in some thoughts about peeling carrots but not green peppers for my list journal. And why was she washing mushrooms like that with a paper towel? I stood quietly for a moment in the doorway.

"Oh, hi, Gabby," Cleo said with a big smile. "I didn't hear you come in."

I was suddenly caught in that itchy space between being angry that Cleo was here when I wasn't expecting her and feeling like I was going to cry because I hated my winter coat that made me look like a boy, even and especially to Debbie Curtis.

I knew I didn't want to cry.

"What are you doing here?" I said, dropping my backpack on the floor. I couldn't put it on the counter where it usually goes, because Cleo had a bowl of raw chicken soaking there.

"Oh." Cleo's smile vanished.

Just then I heard my father's car pull up in the driveway. Cleo put down her cutting knife and hurried out the back way.

"I guess Larry's home," she said — to the air and to the bicycles hanging in the garage, since she was already out the door. Her voice sounded thin and it made me feel bad for what I had said.

At dinner, I sat in self-imposed silence; punishment for being mean to Cleo for no reason. Punishment for looking like a boy. If I wanted something passed to me that I couldn't reach, I did without it. I did without butter on my bread. I did without chicken on my plate.

"Ian's been taking lessons for almost six years." My dad was chatting away. "He started when he was only eight."

My brother didn't bother to correct that particular piece of information. In reality, Ian had picked out the chords to "This Land Is Your Land" when he was only seven years old on one of my dad's old girlfriends' ukulele. My dad left that part out, too.

"He studies with François. You know, that guy over at the college who knew Coltrane?"

My dad usually wasn't too good at regular talking. He never asked to see our homework or who our friends were. Or why I didn't have any. But when it came to discussions about "art" he was downright chatty. And when

Cleo was around he seemed to talk so much you couldn't stop him. He kept on talking about John Coltrane, the famous jazz musician, and Cleo said, "Oh, I *love* John Coltrane. I used to have a roommate who owned lots of his records."

Then Dad said, "Oh, really? Which ones?"

Lately, he was turning into a regular Mr. Upbeat.

I was getting hungry for something more than the steamed vegetables I was pushing around on my plate. I wanted the now-cooked chicken, which smelled like sweet-and-sour, but the platter sat by Cleo's old elbows and I couldn't reach it. I hadn't spoken a word to her since my dad came home. Ian came back an hour later, and half an hour after that we were all there: sitting down like one big, happy something. This was our first all-family-plus-Cleo sit-down meal.

"You look so much like your father," Cleo was saying to Ian. "So you've inherited his artistic talents, as well."

"But my dad's a painter and Ian is a guitar player," I added quickly. And I figured once I had spoken I might as well get to eat.

"Can someone pass me the chicken?" I asked right away.

Cleo handed me the platter. "Well, I meant artistic in general. Ian probably inherited his musical abilities from . . ."

I knew what she was thinking.

She stopped herself, but it was too late.

From your mother, she was going to say. One of the very

few things I knew about my mother — I think but I'm not sure — was that she liked to sing. I knew she had brown hair and little eyes, like me. And I knew her first name was Arlene, because I had her real driver's license in my photo album. But that's about it.

I wondered how Cleo could know anything about my family, but I could tell she did know from the way she stammered.

Cleo regained her composure. ". . . from your mother. Your dad told me your mother liked to sing."

Boy, Cleo really was open. She wasn't afraid to say anything. No one ever mentioned my mother. It was as if the expression "your mother" didn't exist for me. It was only for other people talking about somebody else's mother. I was immune. I was no woman's daughter. I was my daddy's little girl.

End of story.

If Ian heard what Cleo had just said, his face didn't show one sign of it. My dad was just chewing away, like nothing had been said at all. Your mother. It sounded so strange, like she couldn't possibly be talking about me. Everything was quiet.

Too quiet.

So I just blurted out, "Dad, can I get a new winter coat?"

Last winter when Ian ordered a new winter coat from the L. L. Bean catalog, I wanted the same exact one. Last year, I was literally writhing on this very floor begging for a coat just like Ian's.

"You just got a new coat last year, didn't you, Gabby?" My dad was never entirely sure about anything.

Ian didn't say anything, but he rolled his eyes, so obviously *he* remembered. But I hated my coat. It made me look like a boy. And I, for one, could not afford any surplus female disadvantages.

"But *can* I get a new one, Dad?" I asked again, confessing, but not entirely so.

"Let me see this coat you got last year, Gabby," Cleo broke in. "Maybe it's too small already. Did it fit last year?"

I needed no further prompting. I was out of my seat and heading for the coat closet. I returned as the olive drab marshmallow girl, Iditarod contender.

"Whew," Cleo said, looking at me.

Neither my brother nor my father registered that anything was wrong with this picture. The coat fit and was obviously warm.

"There, I knew you got a new coat last year," my dad said.

"But it's so small," I said.

I tried to push my arms out as far as they would go, hoping the sleeves would look too small, but the elastic held tight and the excess of bubble material stretched with me.

But Cleo knew.

"Whew," she said again.

"It looks fine, Gabby," my dad said, satisfied, and he began to clear the dishes.

I was starting to sweat.

"Gabby needs a new coat," Cleo said firmly.

My dad was already in the kitchen washing dishes and putting them right back into the cabinet wet, which I had always thought was normal until I saw a movie one day where a family was washing and then drying their dishes with dish towels. It went on my list.

"We can consign this one," Cleo said. "I'm sure it was expensive. I bet we can even get a nicer one for less than we sell this one for." She spoke louder so my dad could hear as she stared at me and my coat, shaking her head.

We. She had said, "We."

"Whatever you think," the voice came through, over the running water and clanking of plates.

"When?" I asked Cleo.

"Soon," she said, with a smile and a wink. A girl-to-girl wink.

And before I even asked, Cleo added, "This weekend."

Chapter 4

My town sat in the valley of the dark-green lumbering Wallkill River. The Wallkill River flows in the wrong direction. It flows north. Upstream. Against the tide. Away from the ocean. It runs right behind our house.

We learned in science class that the Nile River in Egypt also flows north. I went home and looked it up on the Internet and found out that the Nile is where Miriam from the Bible left her little brother, Moses. Miriam hung around to watch what would happen to him, because her mother told her to.

My mother didn't leave anyone around to watch and see what would happen to me. Maybe she thought she left my brother to look out for me. Boy, was she mistaken.

Our science teacher, Mr. Everett, liked to study the river. He tested water and monitored pollution. He said the river had stories to tell if you knew how to listen. He had us bring in mud samples from the riverbanks and use litmus paper. We counted snapping-turtle eggs.

Mr. Everett wanted all his students to call him by his

first name, George. We all thought that was pretty cool, even if not everyone could bring themselves to actually do it.

"Nobody has turned in their science project sheet," George told the class toward the end of the period. He held up a blank copy to remind us.

I knew I hadn't.

"Come on, people, work with me," George said. "Any medium. Any idea. Any research. Artwork, drama. Just present your ideas for approval." He added, "By the end of class. I'll give you a few moments for quiet reflection on the topic."

A report on the Wallkill River. It was worse than the report on the Huguenot Stone we all did in fifth grade. The Huguenot Stone marked the site of something very old and sat in the center of our town's historic district. It was a huge rock, which was replicated on senior class rings looking exactly like a rock. Teachers loved stuff about our town, claiming the oldest remaining street in America, stone houses, and the deep and slow Wallkill River.

I had no ideas for my project. Most of us sat with our heads perched on our hands, hands bent at the wrist, elbows propped on our desks, staring into space. That's exactly how I was posed when the new girl walked in.

The assistant principal stuck her head into the doorway and looked like something disembodied from a horror movie. Miss Crosby could never seem to bring herself to call George, George. "Excuse me . . . Mr. Everett? This new student is all ready to begin school."

Miss Crosby stepped fully into the room, however cautiously. The new girl stepped in beside her.

George was all ready. He pulled out his plastic glasses and nose, with the eyeballs that bounced out on metal springs.

"Hel-lo new student." George hopped up onto the lab table and bowed like Sir Lancelot.

So here she was, my potential new friend. But I knew as soon as she entered the room that this new girl would be one of "The Ones" before the day was over. She was definitely Amber Whitman material.

The new girl had blond hair. She was thin and walked with the exact female glide I admired but knew I would never master. She had straight white teeth, no braces. (I knew because she was smiling widely at George's Knights of the Round Table routine.) She wore stretchy black pants that flared out at the bottom and a striped top. She wore black platform sneakers and a jacket made of some kind of silver material. She was, in two words, Very Fashionable. I was certain she would be invited to sit at the table with Amber Whitman by lunch today.

Amber wasn't in this science period. She would have to get all the details from her right-hand woman, Kelly Noonan. I could see that Kelly was taking mental notes.

George had gotten down off the lab table and was now doing his "efficient bureaucrat" imitation. He held an invisible clipboard in his hands and pulled an invisible pencil from behind his ear. Miss Crosby pretended not to notice, but her cheeks flared bright red.

"And now, does this new student have a name? Last name first and first name last and middle name middle, please." George cleared his throat purposefully. "Or if you prefer, last middle, middle last, and first first."

George flustered the assistant principal so completely that instead of letting the new girl speak for herself, Miss Crosby stared even more deeply into her clipboard and read from her paperwork.

"Well, there are two new students this week in our middle school. Our AFS student, Lisalotte Verspui and . . . umm . . . Taylor Tyler. No, Tyler Taylor . . . Taylor Such?"

More than a few giggles escaped into the room. It was the combination of George pretending to write down everything that was said and Miss Crosby stammering nervously with the new girl's mixed-up name.

"Taylor Such? Are you supposed to be here or in gym right now?"

Only the new girl wasn't laughing. Her perfect smile was gone.

"Such? Is your last name Such? Or Taylor?" Miss Crosby now searched for answers in her manila folder. "Or Tyler?"

"Ahem, what's your name, New Girl?" George asked formally.

"My name is Taylor Such." The girl spoke in a voice that matched her appearance, both delicate and feminine. "My mother's new last name is Tyler," she said. "Because she's remarried."

"Oh, well that explains that." Miss Crosby regained control. "Taylor Such is the new student," the assistant principal said, and she hurried out the door.

Clearing up the confusion didn't end the laughter. The name "Taylor Such" brought on another wave of snorts and chuckles. Taylor Such was about to cry. George might have been trying to be funny and everyone's pal, but sensitive he was not.

"To such or not to such, that is the question. . . ." George was holding a plastic skull in his open palm when the bell rang.

Taylor hid her face, wet eyes, and was the first one out the door. As I was gathering my books off my desk I looked over at Lynette. Lynette didn't seem to notice anything. She was collecting her things, putting her pencils in size order before zipping her pencil case.

She's coming and she'll cry.

I wonder how Lynette knew.

Chapter 5

Taylor Such was nowhere to be found at lunch that afternoon. As I walked past Amber Whitman's table I could hear Kelly Noonan telling Amber all about the new girl and what happened in George's class.

"She is so weird . . . ," Kelly began.

Kelly leaned over the long Formica table. Kelly Noonan had breasts and, in my opinion, she stuck them out whenever possible. This was one of those occasions.

Maybe if Taylor Such had been in the lunchroom to refute this whole story, if she had been there as living proof that she was not weird, but only shy, things might have turned out differently.

"So weird . . . ," Kelly repeated. "And she is a major show-off." Kelly withdrew her bosom from the table and paused for emphasis.

"You should see what she's wearing. The stupidest shoes I've ever seen in my life." Kelly mocked a horrified scream just as I walked by. "They're like platforms!"

I was so startled I had to steady my hot lunch tray to keep from dropping it.

"And she cried like a baby because everyone heard that her mommy has a new last name," Kelly went on.

I tried to walk very slowly past The Ones' table so I could hear more, but after a few minutes of purposeful feet shuffling I had to move on. I slipped my lunch tray down onto the table beside Patty Parker. When I looked back at Amber, she and her gang were huddled close and laughing. I couldn't understand why they would turn on one of their own.

Taylor appeared again, at recess. In the distance, I saw Miss Crosby urging Taylor out to the playground. She handed Taylor a piece of paper — her schedule, I guessed — and left. Taylor stood by herself, holding her arms tightly around her. She didn't budge except to push up her sleeve, look at her watch, down at her paper, and back at the watch.

That's when Kelly Noonan spotted Taylor. The Ones were stationed at their usual gymnastics spot just inside the football field, next to the shot put and long jump area. Amber Whitman uncurled from a back bend and followed Kelly's pointed finger. Amber nodded as Kelly made the positive identification.

I was able to watch all this from my vantage point under the elm tree, whose roots were completely visible from years of trampling. I had a favorite exposed root that I liked to stand on. I liked to imagine that some early colonial girl had stood on this very spot. I liked to imagine a girl who looked a lot like me but lived in another time, dressed in old-fashioned clothes, and walked down those cobblestone streets, but was somehow going to be my best friend.

I tried to keep my mind away, but my eyes were drawn to what was happening up on the hill. Amber Whitman led the other girls as she marched up the hill toward Taylor Such. Taylor had no idea what she was in for.

I did because I, myself, am a survivor of a dissing experience. It happened the beginning of last fall, not on the playground, but in the gym.

Maybe I should mention something about what I look like. I am not fat or thin. I am kind of tall for a girl in sixth grade. I have dark hair and brown eyes. I turn real brown in the summer. My hair is curly, but it is always in a tight ponytail so it looks straight. I wear the sort of stuff that my brother wears. Jeans and T-shirts (a horribly ugly winter coat), sweatshirts, whatever's comfortable.

I have tried to dress differently. I saw a pleated skirt in a *Seventeen* magazine once, and then by total chance I saw it in the window of a store when I was in New York City visiting my grandfather and step-grandmother. (My mother's mother died five years ago and my grandfather remarried.) Of course, my grandfather made me try it on as soon as I mentioned that I liked it. Or I might have just mentioned that I had seen it somewhere.

Anyway, he had me try it on in the store. It was a little long, but it fit. The skirt was made of a beautiful sheer material that touched softly against my legs, and when I twirled around it lifted into the air. I suddenly had to have this skirt, and my grandfather was so happy to have something to buy me.

But when I got back home and put it on for school I looked terrible. I didn't have the shoes that the girl in the magazine had. I didn't have the sweater. I sure didn't have the face. And I didn't have something else, but I didn't know exactly what that was, exactly.

I just knew I didn't have it.

Girls with mothers have it.

But it was late — the bus would be coming soon — so I wore it anyway. As soon as I got to school wearing my skirt, I couldn't wait to get home. It was like having really bad chapped lips and no Chap Stick. It irritated me the whole day, and I promised myself I'd never try to be a girl again. At least I felt better when, at one o'clock, we changed for gym. So I must have been playing ball a little extra hard. I accidentally hit Melanie Berger in the back of the head with the volleyball, and she was on my team.

"Ow." Melanie dropped instantly.

Amber went rushing to her side. The gym teacher blew her whistle to stop the game and freeze the score.

"I'll get some ice," she announced, and she disappeared through an unidentified door only gym teachers use.

"Gabby, what do you think you're doing? Trying out for the Olympics?!" Amber glared up at me.

Melanie had tears in her eyes. She remained on the

gym floor. Above her head was the sagging volleyball net. The boys in the class immediately took the volleyball and began shooting it through the basketball hoop at the other end of the gym. Lynette wandered off toward the bleachers and sat down facing the wall, counting something.

Kelly and Sophie stepped over from the other side and hovered over the wounded Melanie. Now more than half of The Ones were present and attending to Melanie like they were all Clara Barton. I wanted to say I was sorry. I had wanted to say it right away, but now it was too late.

"What's your problem, anyway?" Kelly started it. She put her hands on her waist and positioned herself in front of me but several feet away. There were bleachers behind me and a wall beside me. Entrapment is a major feature of the "diss-out."

"Is it that stupid skirt you wore today?" Amber joined the attack immediately.

I wonder how it is that someone so mean can be so accurate.

By this point all the girls were circling around me, and most had their hands poised like Kelly's. But it was Amber who did all the talking.

"Gabby Weiss. Do you have to be so angry?"

Then just to prove that girls have to pretend to be nice even when they're being mean, Amber said, "You know, you shouldn't wear a skirt like that, anyway. It just accentuates your hips."

Never before had I given any thought to my hips at all.

I wasn't even sure what "accentuates" meant, or even where my hips were, exactly. But I knew that from that day on I would forever be aware of that particular part of my body.

My fists were clenched. I imagined twisting Amber's arm around her back and locking her in a half nelson until she begged for mercy, which I've only experienced as done to me by my brother.

Instead I said, "Amber, do you have to be a complete asshole? You know, every time you open that mouth of yours it just accentuates your assholeness."

The dissing ended right there, and that was a long time ago, already. Amber and I actually talk to each other now. We did a social studies project together last month when the teacher assigned the groups. We got an A, mostly because of me. Amber Whitman definitely has respect for me.

Anyway, Amber always had another fish to fry, and now it was going to be the new girl.

I watched Taylor up on the hill alone. I saw Amber and her cronies fast approaching. I knew what they had in mind. They already had their arms folded across their chests as they marched.

I also knew Taylor would be crying again by the time they finished telling her off.

Chapter 6

I'm not the heroic type. In fact, I'm not particularly brave at all. I'm afraid of most things; of new things, new places, strangers, of raising my hand with the answer because I'm scared I'll say something stupid. I always forget to think before I talk, and usually I do say something stupid. But in this case I'm glad I didn't think, because I might never have met Taylor.

I got there just as Kelly Noonan was doing the preliminaries.

"What kind of outfit is that?" Kelly asked.

Kelly Noonan always wore one color exclusively. She was in her purple phase. Last year she had gone a full five months in a blue phase.

Today she was wearing faded, purple overalls and a shaggy, purple turtleneck. Since it was unusually warm for November, she wore only a maroon sweater (maroon and white are our school colors) with the varsity letters, NP (for New Paltz), on the back.

"Who do you think you are, dressing up like this is some kind of fashion show?" Kelly continued her interrogation.

Taylor's chin was betraying her with signs of trembling. I had gotten there just in time.

"She thinks she's a girl coming to school and wearing clothing, same as you, Kelly Noonan," I said, stepping into a direct line of fire.

"Figures she'd be your friend," Kelly said. She backed off immediately.

Amber looked right at me. Something in her eyes told me that she wasn't all that bad. She even looked a little scared herself. I realized that if this were all suddenly switched around, Amber Whitman could just as easily be surrounded by some other angry, popular Ones. They could be picking on what she was wearing or what her mother's new last name was or the size of her hips or her breasts or the color of her shoes. Possibly, Amber was realizing this very same thing.

Kelly must have decided telling off Taylor Such wasn't worth this much trouble. She turned and started off down the hill, followed by Melanie and Sophie. Amber stared at the ground, waited a beat, and then abruptly turned and left after her friends.

It was just Taylor and me.

"Thanks," Taylor said, her voice still shaking. She was breathing fast.

"Don't worry about them. They'll all have on your

exact outfit by the end of next week," I told her. "And they'll all want to be your best friend."

It wasn't until I said that out loud that I realized how much I didn't want it to happen.

I was beginning to like Taylor.

"Really?" Taylor smiled.

"Well, maybe." I shrugged.

We started down the hill together. The first bell was ringing.

"So where'd you move from?" I asked.

"New York City," Taylor said. "My dad still lives there."

We both walked the same. Our steps fell right into place. We were about the same size, if you were just looking at things in general. Taylor kept talking a little too quickly, like she was calming herself down.

"We moved here because Richard got a great job and the real estate market here is about to boom."

"Richard is your stepfather?" I asked.

"Oh, Richard is great," Taylor said, even though I hadn't asked if she liked him or not. "I knew him since way before my parents got divorced. He was already like family." Taylor got to the door and I held it open.

She walked through and stopped just inside the hall.

I glanced at her schedule. "This way." I pointed.

We walked down the hall together while everyone else was rushing to their classes.

"Hi, Gabby." Peter passed us.

I waved.

Amber was coming the other way. She was alone.

"Hi, Gabby." She nodded at me and then said to Taylor, "Hi, Taylor."

I had known Taylor less than a day, but it felt okay to kind of bang into her with my shoulder. "See," I said with a big, everything-is-okay grin. "I told you."

Taylor smiled and leaned back into my push.

Chapter 7

Taylor called me that very night and invited me to her house the next day after school. I didn't need a bus note because Mrs. Tyler and Taylor's stepfather, Richard Tyler, lived in one of the old historic houses near the school and we would walk. Taylor told me it was Richard who advised her parents to buy their co-op on the upper west side of New York City. That was when her parents first were married, so when they got divorced and had to sell it they made a fantastic profit. Her father stayed in New York City. Taylor said Richard was amazing at foreseeing property trends. I supposed that was good for New Paltz, real estate–wise, anyway.

A cold front was definitely moving in from wherever they move in from, but I was determined to hold out until I went shopping with Cleo over the weekend. My winter coat was now unbearably ugly and therefore unwearable. Instead, I wore a lot of layers and a wool hat. Taylor and I crossed over the football field with our backpacks weighing us down. We would have to cut through the Dunkin' Donuts parking lot, over the empty lot where there's a hole in the chain-link fence, and up the hill to Taylor's neighborhood.

The Dunkin' Donuts parking lot was nearly empty. The smell of sugar leaked out the back of the building through the roar of loud ventilators and an open rear door.

"I love the chocolate glaze," Taylor said and sniffed the air.

She looked so funny; her nose pointing up, her backpack hanging down, the cold air coming out with her words like the steam from the Dunkin' Donuts exhaust — I started to laugh. A real laugh, the kind you can't stop.

Taylor looked at me a minute and then she said it again — "I looove the chocolate glaze" — in this exaggerated voice.

She broke out laughing, too. We laughed so long our stomachs hurt. We had reached the vacant lot and climbed through the fence, our laughter reduced to a few uncontrollable spasms now and then. Until I said it — "I love the chocolate glaze"— and we started all over again. All the way to her house.

Mrs. Tyler opened the door before we even got there, as though she was expecting something new. Then I realized it must be me.

I was laughing so much my voice was kind of louder and hoarser than it usually is. My eyes were probably watery and my cheeks were probably blotchy. I had this stupid leftover laughing smile on my face.

"You must be Gabby," Mrs. Tyler said, still standing in the doorway so we had to stop on the front step and wait.

"Uh-huh," I said. Loudly.

"C'mon, Mom. Just let us come in first," Taylor said. She was slipping her backpack off. Taylor's mother took it from her and then let us in.

I watched Taylor carefully. There was something here that was signaling me to be aware, a test. It was one of those situations where I was deficient as a girl, a girl who otherwise would have understood what was expected of her.

Taylor took off her shoes. So I did, too. There were two other pairs of shoes already there. I placed my sneakers beside Taylor's. (Taylor hadn't worn her platforms that day, but I was still betting some One would have an identical pair by the end of the next week.)

I felt Mrs. Tyler's eyes on my back. I switched my sneakers around so they were lined up left then right, both pointing in like the others, and I stood up.

"Would you like a little snack, girls?" Mrs. Tyler asked. She was very tall. And thin. She had blond hair, too, though not as blond as Taylor's.

"Thanks, Mom," Taylor answered. I decided it would be best to not say anything, so that I couldn't say the wrong thing.

But that was the wrong thing. "Would you like something to eat, Gabby?" she asked me.

This was more than a test.

"Sure," I answered.

This was a minefield.

"Sure, please," I added.

36

We followed Mrs. Tyler into the kitchen, single file. Taylor looked back at me and smiled. She raised her eyebrows luringly and, just before she was seen, stuck out her tongue at her mother.

I wanted to smile at Taylor's joke, but I was too awestruck by her home.

It looked to me that everything in Taylor's house was white. The walls were white. The rugs were white. The sofa in the living room, where, Taylor told me, no one was allowed to stand for more than a few moments to admire, was white. The leather couches in the den where the TV was were the color of perfectly mashed potatoes. The bathroom was filled with white towels, Dove soap, white curtains, and chrome.

Even Taylor and her mother looked white in that house, with their blond hair and creamy skin. I felt dark, big, and too loud and clumsy.

The more uncomfortable I felt, the more I acted dark and big, too loud and clumsy. Just like when I was in third grade and I was invited to Beth Moore's birthday party. The whole memory is a blur, like a photograph that's out of focus. I do remember jumping on Beth Moore's couch, and I remember when Beth told me I wasn't allowed to come to her house anymore.

To credit her eight-year-old politeness, Beth didn't actually volunteer the information. It didn't come out for two whole days, when at school I asked Beth if she wanted to play on the playground with me.

We had just come out for recess, and I had my eye on

something just past the sandbox. The two best swings were still empty.

"Do you want to play with me, Beth?" I asked.

Beth said, "My mom says you can't come to my house again."

It took my eight-year-old brain a few minutes to figure out what she was saying. But I did figure it out. Beth's mother had banned me from her house.

"What are you talking about?" I asked Beth, as if I was really annoyed, instead of horribly embarrassed and tremendously sad.

"My mom said you were too wild and you jumped on our couches." Beth looked down at the ground. She flicked a little rock around with the tip of her sneaker.

I knew then, as much as I liked Beth Moore (and as much as Beth liked me), we weren't going to be friends.

"I was just asking you if you wanted to swing," I snapped. "But now, forget it."

"I'm sorry," Beth said, still looking at her feet.

Not as sorry as I was. Still, I was glad I wouldn't be going to her house again. I didn't know mothers could disapprove of and dislike one little girl so much. I never thought anyone noticed me at all. But from then on, I knew I had to be more careful, had to watch my step.

And here I was, watching my step. Steps I hadn't been taught to take.

At the Tylers' house food was only allowed in the dining room. Mrs. Tyler put out milk (white!) and cookies (also white). Each cookie had delicate stripes of chocolate across the top and a hole in the center, so you could put it on your finger and spin it.

I started to nibble my cookie as it spun on the tip of my finger but quickly decided against this method of eating. I didn't know if Mrs. Tyler had seen me yet or not.

I had this feeling Mrs. Tyler didn't like me, already. It was something about the way she looked at me later, when Taylor and I were playing Monopoly in the family room. I got a little carried away making jokes about the car and the top hat, and I was a little loud, again. Mrs. Tyler walked by just as I said "brang" instead of "brought," and she corrected me. My dad had always corrected me on that, too, and I hadn't done it for years until, of course, just then.

My dad was supposed to pick me up on his way home from the university, and around five o'clock I heard him beep his horn. I could tell Mrs. Tyler didn't approve of that, either.

"My dad's here," I said, moving to get my shoes on.

"Yes, I hear the beeping."

"Well, Thursdays are his student critiques and he's probably real tired," I explained (I lied — his crits were on Wednesdays), and then at the same time I felt further inclined to entice Mrs. Tyler with something interesting about me.

"And he gets up at five thirty in the morning to paint, so he's extra, extra tired."

"Oh, what kind of paintings does your father do?" she asked me.

"Oil paintings. Landscapes mostly. Cows and clouds and stuff," I said.

I looked up from the floor, where I was busy tying my laces, to see if I had made an impression. From this angle Mrs. Tyler seemed immense. Looming tall. But yes, she seemed interested.

"Well, Gabby, it was nice to meet you," she said, opening the door. "We'll see you again soon, I hope."

"Bye, Gabby," Taylor said. "See you tomorrow in school."

I remembered to say "Thank you for having me" to Mrs. Tyler, and right before I got into my dad's car I turned to Taylor and said, "I loove the chocolate glaze."

Taylor laughed. Mrs. Tyler looked puzzled. I saw Taylor turn inside her house without explaining the joke to her mother. Maybe this time it wouldn't matter what her mother thought of me.

Chapter 8

I was studying Cleo as we drove to the new mall in Poughkeepsie. With her arms bent and her hands on the steering wheel, Cleo's elbows did not look so wrinkled. She wore a thin line of brown eyeliner on her upper lids, a pale lip gloss, and other than that nothing that I could detect. Cleo wasn't the makeup kind. She wasn't the dress-up kind, either, which was funny since she designed clothing. Cleo had her own line of shirts and pants with her drawings on the arms or legs or in the center of her sack-of-potatoes dresses (there was no other way to describe them). Mostly she had pictures of leaves or tree branches or what looked like animal bones on her clothing. All natural things that you might find walking through the woods.

Cleo had given me one of her T-shirts the first time I met her. The T-shirt had tiny falling leaves on the sleeve and one on the front like it had just landed there by accident. But I left it in gym once and someone stole it. I was afraid to tell Cleo, but so far she hadn't asked why I never wear that shirt. Now, driving to the mall, it seemed like years ago, though it was probably just about ten months before I first met Cleo. I suppose I was getting used to her.

"Maybe there'll be some of those ladies with baskets giving out free stuff right by the door," I said. I stopped staring at Cleo. We were getting close to the mall now.

There was a Saks Fifth Avenue at this mall that Cleo said would probably have lots of winter coats on sale. She said by November the stores are getting rid of their winter stuff and getting ready for the mid-winter cruise crowd, as in ocean liners to the Caribbean. Whatever.

"Oh, goody. You mean those women who squirt you with perfume when you walk by?" Cleo scrunched up her face.

"Yeah, the ones that look like mannequins when they stand still." I thought that was a good one.

"You mean the ones who wear so much makeup their own mothers wouldn't recognize them without it?" Cleo said.

I laughed and was thinking of something to add. It felt like we were friends or even something more. Right away I could feel my heart start thumping. I always say something dumb when I get like this.

But Cleo had stopped smiling. And I hadn't even said anything dumb yet.

"I'm so sorry," she said quietly. She had her hand over her mouth.

"What? What?" I looked out the window and then back at Cleo.

"I can't believe I said that," she said. "I'm sorry."

In my mind I flashed over the last few words Cleo had said. *Their own mothers*, she had said, but it meant nothing to me. *Their own mothers* — these are words that just get tossed around and immediately evaporate in the air.

"Why?" I asked. "Sorry for what?"

"I guess everyone just assumes you have a mother, don't they?" Cleo explained. "And I'm sorry for the other night at dinner. It's just that I thought if I didn't finish what I was going to say about your mother it would have been worse."

Cleo looked sad. "Oh, I always say something dumb."

"So do I!" I nearly shouted. I couldn't believe I had just been thinking the same thing. She was like me. I was like Cleo.

"I mean, you didn't say anything dumb," I said quickly. "It doesn't bother me. People always say things like that, like 'Go tell your mother.' Or 'Wait till your mother finds out.' Or 'Your mother will be so proud.' . . . Like teachers or strangers or nurses, stuff like that." Once I had started, I couldn't stop talking.

Talking but not feeling anything. All words, information I was used to imparting, information that usually got people to feel sorry for me. Sometimes it got me out of trouble, sometimes it got me out of having to do stuff.

"The only thing . . . ," I began.

And if feeling sorry for me got Cleo to like me, I'd take that, too.

"The only thing that kind of bothers me . . . is

Mother's Day," I told Cleo. "I have this whole collection of dried-up marigolds in green plastic planters from school."

But that was true. Mother's Day bothered me, if I thought about it. I used to give the Mother's Day gifts to my Nana, but after she died I started hiding them in the back of my closet. I don't know why I didn't just throw them away. Anyway, they stopped having us make Mother's Day projects by second grade. It was just cards now, and cards are easier to get rid of. Mother's Day still came and went every year. Come to think about it, I hated Mother's Day.

Cleo was listening. She looked interested, but she looked sad. I was giving too much away, thinking too little and talking too much. I should have stopped, but Cleo looked like she wanted me to keep going. To keep talking. Once I realized this it all came out at once.

"Cleo?" I blurted out. "Do you think I have big hips?"

At first I couldn't tell if Cleo had sneezed or laughed real loud. "Who told you that?" she asked.

When I didn't answer, Cleo said seriously, "Gabby, you are looking less like a little girl and more like a woman."

I couldn't tell if that was good or bad. "Does that mean I do?"

"No. You certainly don't have big hips!" Cleo said firmly. "These are good changes. It means you'll be a woman soon." She paused.

"Unless you already are?" Cleo asked deliberately.

What did she mean? Did she mean what I thought she meant? Like in the movie from health class? Me?

"Oh, no," I said. "Not me." The mall was just ahead, thank goodness.

"Well now, here we are. Let's go find you the perfect coat!" she said as she pulled the car into a parking space. "Something as beautiful as you are."

The first thing we saw when we walked through the big glass doors of Saks Fifth Avenue was two women poised like models — tall, wearing lots of lipstick and eye shadow, with little baskets slung over their arms. Cleo and I hurried right by them, trying to hold in our chuckles, but neither one of them tried to spray us with anything. How they could just *see* that we weren't the typical Saks Fifth Avenue–shopper types, I didn't know.

We rode up the escalator to the Young Miss department on the second floor. Cleo was right. There were displays of shorts and sandals and summer dresses and hats. And way in the back were rows and rows of coats with big signs saying 25% OFF, so crammed together they held themselves up off the floor without hangers.

Cleo picked through the coats like a clothing expert, which of course she was. She could tell right away what would fit or not fit, what was a maybe and what was out of the question.

"Oh my God, no. You'd look like one of those poofy ice skaters in that thing," she said, when I held up a short, pinkish jacket trimmed with white fur around the sleeves and the hood.

And Cleo knew what was *me* and what wasn't. Which was more than I had ever figured out before.

No. No. Maybe. No. Maybe. Definitely no.

I was getting hot and tired of trying on coats. Back to the first maybe. It was a simple black-and-red winter parka that was cinched just a little at the waist to give it shape. The saleslady came bustling over.

"This is the one," Cleo said to the woman and then turned to me. "Right?"

"Yup," I said.

"Come over here and I'll ring you up," the saleslady said with an irritated look on her face. She, too, must have been able to tell we weren't the big Saks Fifth Avenue–shopper types. She was ready to make the sale and move on.

The woman's voice trailed away as she whisked the coat over to the cash register. "You and your daughter have made an excellent choice," she said.

These words lingered in the air, as if waiting to be noticed. Cleo laid her credit card on the counter with a snapping sound. Then she looked right at me and smiled.

"Yes," she said. "We have."

Chapter 9

My brand-new coat was hanging in the hall closet, waiting for Monday to be worn to school. And I was waiting; a too-long, boring weekend. I knew Taylor wasn't going to be around, not even to talk with on the phone. She had left Friday to go visit her dad in New York City (and that was a long-distance call). Cleo left just after our shopping trip for a clothing show somewhere in Connecticut. It was just going to be me and my dad and my brother all weekend.

And my dad was spending practically the whole weekend out in his studio painting. It seemed that lately, like for the last several months, like for as long as Cleo's been around, Dad's been painting a lot. And whistling a lot. My dad whistles really good when he's in a good mood.

I watched TV mostly, although we don't have cable out here, something to do with the wet ground and the closeness of the river, and my dad is too cheap to buy one of those satellite things. So we have an antenna, and no one I talk to even knows what an antenna is.

Sunday my brother and I were on the two couches in

the living room. I was lying down. Ian was sitting up with his guitar. Ian, of course, had the remote control. He never lets me even touch the controller when he's watching something. Ian had on some science-fiction movie, and he was practicing scales during commercials.

"Do you have to do that?" I said. I turned my head to him, but other than that I didn't move my body at all. My feet stuck up into my view of the movie, but I didn't care. I wasn't even paying attention.

"It's a commercial," he answered. His fingers were lifting and pressing down all over the neck of his guitar, so fast they couldn't possibly know what they were do-ing. His other hand seemed barely to move over the hole in the center, but notes were coming out, like millions of beads forever dropping on the floor.

"It's not a commercial now," I complained.

"You're not even watching," Ian said to me.

"I am, too."

After a beat I added, "Why can't you do that in your room?"

He didn't answer, but it seemed to me he played louder after that. When the movie was finally over, I held out my hand for the controller.

"Now it's my turn," I said. We each were allowed sixty minutes for TV choice a day. That was Ian's rule. Some-times, he'd rack up minutes from the day before and add them to his time the next day or even the next week. When I'd say that wasn't fair, he'd say I could do it, too, only I could never keep track of something like that.

"No, it isn't," Ian informed me. "I've got twenty-three minutes left over from last Tuesday."

"Ian. It's my turn to pick a show," I said. The only response I received was a jazzy riff on the guitar but no controller.

I cannot say that on other occasions I had not thrown myself completely into the fight, beginning with a few whines then moving onto a fierce lunge for the controller. Throwing a pillow, yelling for my father, or worse. But that day I didn't have it in me. The weekend was almost over. I just wondered why Ian had to be so mean to me. Why he couldn't, or wouldn't, just want to make me happy one time. Like the families on the TV shows. Just like that. Just to be nice.

I decided to walk away. Ian sat still playing, the guitar between his heart and his lap like a shield. He still didn't offer me my turn.

The music that came out of his guitar seemed just as distant. Far away from me. Where did it come from? Why had he inherited something from a mother who liked to sing?

And what about me?

As I left the room, I thought I heard his voice.

"Here, take the dumb controller."

I went downstairs and played video games by myself till my thumbs ached. I went back upstairs to the kitchen and stared into the pantry, but there was nothing to eat.

I wasn't hungry anyway. I wandered outside for no other reason than I had nothing better to do than watch acorns fall from the trees and I didn't feel like working on my science project.

Acorns were dropping so fast it was like someone was throwing them. One hit me square in the neck.

"Ow." I spun around and rubbed the spot behind my ear.

But acorns don't fall sideways.

"Knock it off," I shouted into the empty yard.

No one was there, but I knew. Throwing acorns was Ian's signature move.

Another acorn flew by my right shoulder. Now he was asking for it. I ran around the side of the house by the cellar door. As I ran I grabbed as many fallen nuts from the ground as I could. I zigzagged back and forth, which I knew from experience made me a moving target, harder to hit. Only one more acorn landed on the back of my leg before I reached cover. Once I was safely behind the house I thrust the acorns into my pockets and filled my fists with more. I peered around the house.

Ian was in his favorite spot. He liked to climb to the top of our old swing set and strategically straddle the bar across the slide. He couldn't run anywhere, but, of course, he had a clear view of me from almost anywhere in the yard, and his aim was better so it didn't matter.

I decided on a surprise attack. I hated to get spiderwebs in my face, but that's just what Ian counted on. Instead of running across the lawn, I would go around the other side of the house, crawl under the porch, and get off at least my one or two shots before Ian could turn around. (Our rule had always been only one acorn at a time; heaving a whole handful was not allowed. And not in the face.)

"C'mon in! Supper!"

It was our dad. He had come out onto the porch. If Ian turned around now he would see my hiding place. I withdrew deeper into the spiderwebs. They stuck to my fingers and my hair, but I didn't make a sound.

Ian jumped down off the swing set and headed inside, right toward me. But I could still leap out as he walked by. At close range I might even hit him for once. I saw Ian's feet pass. I waited. Five . . . four . . . three . . . two . . .

"Ha! Gotcha!" Ian bent down and saw me, crouched under the porch, where I was defenseless.

He had his acorn poised and ready to throw, but he didn't.

"I knew you were there all the time," Ian said. He emptied the rest of his ammunition onto the ground and headed inside for dinner.

"Just as long as you know I'm the best," he said.

Sometimes Ian came just close enough to being nice to me that I could see some potential.

Chapter 10

Monday morning I woke before my alarm even went off. I dressed fast, ate, and went outside wearing my brand-new, beautiful coat. Ready to go to school. All ready. However, I was now twenty-two minutes early for the bus.

I was so early that it was still dark out. I followed the little path my dad cut in the tall grass toward the water. I looked at my watch. Twenty-one minutes to go. I walked a little farther. Darkness sat so deeply on the river that everything was the same color — the sky, the ground, and the slow-moving Wallkill. It felt like the sun would not be able to rise up and lift it away.

I stood with my feet tipped down toward the water. My heels were dug into the steep wall of mud, and that was the only thing that kept me from slipping into the river. A cold wind came across the valley and whipped my hair across my face. It got caught in my mouth and stung my eyes. I usually wore my hair back so tightly that a tornado couldn't blow a strand out of place. But on our way out of the department store Friday, Cleo had insisted on buying me these two barrettes. They sparkled with pink-and-blue-and-yellow light. They were small crystal-butterfly barrettes. One for each side of my head, perched just above my temples — butterflies alighting for a brief rest before taking off in flight. That's how Cleo described them, anyway.

"Well, try wearing your hair down," Cleo had said when I told her I didn't wear barrettes.

I wear a ponytail, always. But she bought them for me anyway, for some possible me I couldn't see. In the store I was hopeful, but here and now I anticipated these barrettes having the same fate as the skirt my grandfather had bought me.

Now I watched the murky river. Trees on the opposite bank struggled to stay part of the land. They leaned dangerously over the passing river. Huge roots stuck out from the bank, like giant hands reaching for something to grab onto as the dirt they stood on was drained away.

George told us that the river pulls soil from the far side of its path and drops sediment on the other, and so it slowly creates bends and turns as it travels on its way. But slowly, ever so slowly. It took thousands of years to make this Wallkill River Valley; to flatten the land by meandering back and forth. Thousands of years, going nowhere, just wearing away at the same piece of land until it was flat, until it was a valley.

I reached up and touched my hair, to touch the barrettes, to pull the hair from my face. My hair had doubled in size, and it blew around my head, out of my

53

control. I slipped one butterfly from my hair and then the other. I bent down in the wet mud, careful not to get it on my new coat. With a strong stick I started digging.

When the hole looked big enough I dropped the two barrettes in and quickly covered them up. Still kneeling beside the burial spot, I pulled my hair back with one hand and flipped a hair tie around it with the other. I tugged it all into a tight ponytail.

I was me again. The old me, the one I was used to.

I saw my bus in the far distance across the flats, just rounding the corner by the Johnsons' farm. If I ran I would just make it.

Chapter 11

After almost a whole week wearing my new coat, it didn't feel new anymore. Taylor didn't feel new anymore, either. We were friends. We claimed the very end of one table in the cafeteria for ourselves.

"Do you think this weekend you could sleep over at my house?" Taylor asked me. She brought lunch from home and was opening various wrapped items and setting them out before her.

Somewhere in the back of my head I thought I was supposed to ask Taylor to my house next, since I had been to her house once already. But I didn't want to. I liked Taylor's house, even if I didn't feel completely welcomed. Her house had what mine was missing. It was where I wanted to belong.

I even had a dream about it one night that week. I couldn't remember it all, but it was sort of my house/Taylor's house, and I was sleeping in my dream, which is always strange. Mrs. Tyler was saying, "Wake up, sleepyhead. Wake up," in this soft voice. I woke up in my dream, but I knew I was still dreaming, and in my dream

I knew Mrs. Tyler wasn't talking to me. When I really woke up I had real tears in my eyes and my pillow was all wet, but I don't remember crying in my dream.

"So can you sleep over?" Taylor repeated. "I already asked my mom if you could."

"Sure," I said. I was having the chicken taco boat, applesauce, carrot sticks, and milk.

"Don't you have to ask your mom first?" Taylor asked.

I answered, as I always did before I was ready to explain, "She'll let me."

"Good, because this is my weekend with my mom. And Richard is going away for business. Not that you wouldn't like Richard, because he's the best."

Taylor took a slip from her bottle of V8. "But when it's just us girls, it's really special. I really want you to come."

I could tell she meant it. Taylor said things just as she felt them, sort of like Cleo.

"It will be so much fun," Taylor said.

"Your mom said I could come over?" I had to ask. "Sleep over?"

"Of course, silly. Why?"

"I don't know. I thought maybe she didn't like me," I ventured.

"Who cares what she thinks?" Taylor said, flipping her hair off her shoulder.

Yeah, who cares? I thought, and I pushed away the feeling of hurt that was threatening to sting me. *Who cares?*

"What did you do last weekend in New York?" I said, to change the topic.

"My dad took me to a movie and we went out to dinner, and that's really depressing because you look around
and there're all these other kids eating out with just their
dads, ordering Shirley Temples, and you just know
they're divorced, too."

Taylor was opening her dessert. Four cookies wrapped
in waxed paper.

"But the divorce was really the best thing. They both
say so. I want my mom to be happy, and she's so happy
with Richard."

Taylor offered me two of her cookies.

"Thanks," I said.

"My mom always packs me too much to eat," Taylor
said, biting into her dessert. "Why do you always buy?"

My mouth was full. The cookie was more crumbly
than I had anticipated, so after I took a bite I had to shove
it all in my mouth or else have it fall onto the table.

"Mmmfff." I tried to swallow.

"Got milk?" Taylor laughed as she handed me my
container.

If I laughed the cookie was going all over the place. I
thought that would be more unsightly than either of my
two previous choices. I breathed in through my nose
slowly and took a swig of milk. My cheeks were stuffed
full and milk dripped on my chin.

Taylor was hysterical. "You should see you!" she
squealed.

I finally swallowed. I wiped my face. I looked at Taylor
and said with a big smile, "I looove the chocolate glaze."

We both nearly burst with laughter.

As soon as we gained control of ourselves, Taylor said, "Got milk?"

"I looove the chocolate glaze," I said on cue.

And just like that we had a history. Two lines only we two understood.

And then I said, "I didn't really tell you the truth before, Taylor. I don't have a mother."

Taylor stopped laughing and looked at me, waiting for me to finish explaining. She didn't know that I was already finished.

"What do you mean? Are your parents divorced?"

"My mother died when I was three." It was my standard response.

Unless someone went further — and they usually never did — I never elaborated. Most people said a polite "Oh, I'm sorry" and that was it. But just in case, I had a prepared second response.

"How did she die?" Taylor went further.

"It was an accident." I had to use my prepared second response.

Taylor's face looked twisted. She didn't say anything more. She did something more amazing. I was just about to carry my tray to the garbage, and she reached out and touched my hand.

"I don't even remember her," I said, like lines from a play.

"Oh," Taylor said sadly. She shook her head back and forth. "An accident," she said softly to herself.

"Let's go out," I stood up. "There's only a little bit of recess left."

"Okay." Taylor stuffed everything into her bag.

Most of the kids had already finished and left. The only full table still sitting was the table of boys. They were usually the first to throw their food across the table, shout, yell, leave garbage all over, and run outside. Then I saw the cafeteria lady watching them with her eagle eye from a swivel chair by the door. The whole boys' table must have gotten lunch detention. Peter sat at that table.

As we passed by the boys on our way out, Taylor said loudly, "Got milk?"

"I looove the chocolate glaze," I answered back equally as loud.

"You guys are so ditzy," Peter said to us. He tried to blow his straw paper at us as we scooted by.

"So are you," Taylor and I said at the exact same time. Peter leaped from his seat like he was going to chase us.

"There will be absolutely no communicating!" The cafeteria lady swooped down from her observation perch.

Laughing wildly, we ran for the door before she could give us detention.

"Quick, head for the hills," I said, laughing. I felt the rush and fear of being chased. Taylor was right behind me.

As we stepped into the cold air and it was quiet, I realized I had let Taylor think I meant "an accident," like a car accident or something. An accident — I had let her think I didn't have anything to do with my mother's death.

But it was *an accident*, I told myself, so I hadn't really been lying.

Chapter 12

*F*riday there was an assembly. The auditorium was loud, filled with the noise of kids talking and teachers trying to talk over it. Everyone was up and down, sitting and then standing, signaling for friends. Classes filed down each row. Boys leaped over seats to be next to or away from someone, or to sneak out altogether. Peter was just ahead of me in my row, sidling down the aisle.

I spotted Taylor with her fourth-period social studies class, the only class we didn't have together except for Spanish. I waved my hands around but she didn't see me. She was moving along the seats four or five rows behind. The lights were starting to dim, so I pulled my seat out and sat down.

It got pitch-black in the auditorium, and slowly the sounds from the audience quieted. Eventually the *Shhs* and *Shushes* and *Be quiets* stopped, too. African drumming music rose into the air. The lights onstage came up on two white-gloved hands that seemed to move without a body. As the music got louder, a large, colorful mask became visible in the darkness. Then someone started screaming.

At first I thought it was part of the show. But soon there was an uncomfortable rustling from the people around me, voices whispering and I had a feeling that something was not right. The music kept on playing, and the hands and mask moved around on the stage in their native dance. More and more hands appeared, but the screaming didn't stop. It turned into loud sobs and crying, one shriek then another.

The din from the audience was louder now. Disorder was erupting. I turned to Peter, who was sitting next to me.

"What's going on?" I asked him.

"I don't know." He didn't even have to whisper; everyone was talking now. "I think someone got scared."

Just then we all saw Lynette Waters being escorted up the aisle by Mr. Salinger, the principal, followed by Lynette's two friends and a teacher. Lynette was crying and had her hands over her ears. A sliver of bright light pierced the darkness as the back doors were opened to let them out, and then all was dark again. The music, which had stopped, suddenly began, and the masks and hands began dancing once more.

"What the heck was that all about?" Peter said to me when it was nearly quiet again.

"Lynette knows things other people don't," I whispered back.

"I think she's just retarded from being hit by a truck."

"Don't say that."

"Say what?" Peter asked.

A loud "Shhh" came down our way. Peter made a funny, mock-angry face back into the blackness where that sound had come from. It made me giggle. (Funny, because I am definitely not the giggling type.) I clamped my hand over my mouth, and we both turned to watch the stage.

By the end of the day, the speculation had stopped and no one even mentioned the screaming incident anymore, though Lynette didn't return to class before the school day ended at two thirty-five.

This was the day I was going to Taylor's for a sleepover. I had my overnight stuff in my backpack; my toothbrush, a comb, a handful of hair bands, pajamas, clean underwear, socks, and a fresh T-shirt.

Mrs. Tyler wasn't waiting at the door this time. She wasn't even home. After knocking and ringing, Taylor let herself in with a key that was hidden in a fake rock with a secret compartment.

"She said she might be working," Taylor said.

"What does she do?" I asked, stepping inside. I pretended the house was familiar already; that I lived there, too.

"She's an interior designer but she doesn't get paid, yet." Taylor flung off her shoes in two different directions. One hit the wall. "That's why she's so fussy about the house."

"I'm home, Mom," Taylor shouted. "Here's my coat!" She threw it on the floor.

"I thought you said . . ." I felt a quick panic.

"No, don't worry. She's not here. I'm just being wild and free," Taylor said. Then she quickly straightened out her shoes and hung up both our coats. "But not that free. . . ."

"Let's have a snack on the couch in front of the TV before she gets home," Taylor said. Her eyes widened. Her eyebrows lifted. I was learning that was Taylor's sign for misbehavior.

We plopped down on the white leather couch, our hands holding big glasses of milk and the entire box of Chips Ahoy between us. Taylor threw me the controller with the glee of a prisoner just let out of jail.

"You pick," she said.

We dunked the cookies in the milk and flipped through every channel.

"Hey, what was that?" Taylor said and pointed. She wanted me to stop on MTV.

"I'll go back," I said, but as I deftly pushed the button on the controller I knocked my glass over and milk spilled onto the seat beside me, one cookie floating in the puddle it created.

"Oh, no!" I cried at the exact same moment we heard the front door swing open.

"Hello? Taylor? It's Mommy." It was Mrs. Tyler's voice. "Are you home?"

In the single second, Taylor leaped up from her spot and then sat directly down again into the pool of white. When her mother turned the corner into the living room Taylor was smiling pleasantly, the spill completely covered.

"Taylor, you know I don't like you eating in here." Mrs. Tyler frowned when she saw the glasses and the empty cookie box.

"Oh, sorry, Mommy. I know," Taylor said. "But we are being so careful."

"Hello, Gabby," Mrs. Tyler said as she turned to me.

"Hi," I said. I was so afraid of what might happen next. I was wondering how much milk Taylor's jeans could absorb if she had to stand up.

"Well, I'm going to change," Mrs. Tyler said. She headed down the hall to her bedroom. "Please, don't make a habit of this," she called back.

"We won't," Taylor shouted. Then she quickly jumped up. The milk was gone, for the most part. The cookie was stuck to the seat of her pants.

"Hurry, get a paper towel," Taylor whispered, and she ran into her room.

Chapter 13

By the time Mrs. Tyler came back, the milk was gone, the glasses were in the dishwasher, and Taylor was in a new pair of pants.

"So how was school?" Mrs. Tyler asked us both later, when we were in the kitchen eating dinner. I could tell she meant me, too, because she looked right at me when she asked.

"Good," I answered.

"Taylor, did you get your vocabulary test back?"

"Mom, you know I did," Taylor said, slipping her napkin onto her lap.

I did the same. Napkin in lap.

"You already looked in my binder," Taylor continued. "You know I got an eighty-two."

"You lost points on spelling," Mrs. Tyler said between chewing. Mrs. Tyler ate more slowly than anyone I had ever seen, as if she didn't really enjoy it. She set her fork down on the edge of her plate after almost every bite. I almost never put down my fork till I am done eating.

But I did then.

After we finished eating and had cleaned up, Mrs. Tyler announced we were having ice cream sundaes for our just-the-girls night. She put out two kinds of ice cream — vanilla and coffee — and three toppings — hot fudge, chocolate crunchies, and whipped cream. She made Taylor wait until I had made my sundae before she could eat hers. Maybe Mrs. Tyler was liking me a little more. Or maybe that's just another thing girls have to do — wait till everyone is served before eating. Then Mrs. Tyler made herself one, too. A huge one. And we all dug in. Three girls eating lots of ice cream.

Mrs. Tyler turned to me. I got ready.

"Gabby, I read about your father in the paper this week," she said. She smiled. She looked so much like Taylor, I could see, not just her hair. When she smiled, she had the same squinty-eyed smile.

"I read that he's in the faculty art show," Mrs. Tyler told me.

"Oh, yeah," I said, but it was the first I had heard of it.

It upset me that Mrs. Tyler knew more than I did about my father.

"The opening is in two weeks. Are you going?" she asked me.

As she spoke I had this clear image of standing before a painting, a single brush stroke across this huge canvas. It was a long time ago at a gallery opening. I was looking up at this enormous, empty painting, while my dad stood next to me and explained its place in postmodern history. It almost made sense to me the way he said it, and I stood for a moment taking it all in, trying to understand. I reached up to take my dad's hand. But it wasn't my dad! While I had been thinking, my dad had walked away and someone else was standing there. I was holding the hand of some total stranger.

I must have had that same lost look on my face; I wasn't listening to what Mrs. Tyler had just said.

"Is the gallery open to the public, do you know?" Mrs. Tyler asked, and, by the way, she sounded as if she had tried more than one time.

"Oh, yeah. Anyone can go," I said. "You should come."

"Yes, I'd love to." Mrs. Tyler took another scoop of ice cream and drizzled hot fudge all over it.

"Ice cream is my one weakness," she said, licking the spoon.

I could believe that one. Mrs. Tyler didn't seem to have many weaknesses.

Chapter 14

Taylor and I lay in bed that night, in the darkness, talking. Taylor's bedroom (which I hadn't gotten to see on my first visit) was perfect. It was symmetrical. Two twin beds, one on each side of the room, exactly the same distance from the walls; matching bedspreads that also matched the curtains; two white, warm rugs for our feet when we stepped out of bed; tightly tucked blankets to keep us under the covers like little pastries.

After dinner, after some more TV and a little time on the computer, Mrs. Tyler had told us to go to bed. No talking. It was late. We brushed our teeth, frothing our mouths full of toothpaste and making faces in the mirror.

Taylor used the toilet first while I waited in her room, carefully sitting on the bed, afraid to pull down the covers until I saw Taylor do it.

"Your turn," Taylor said when she came into the room.

I got up and went into the bathroom. When I finished and came out, Taylor was hanging upside down. She was lying across the bed on her back and her head was nearly touching the floor, her hair spread out loosely like it was floating underwater.

"Look at this," she called. She covered the top half of her head, her eyes and nose, with her hand. "Pretend this is right-side up and my chin is the top of my head."

It took me a while to get what she was doing. Taylor kept talking, reciting the Gettysburg Address, exaggerating her mouth movements. Finally her face started to look like a long, bald head with no eyes and a crooked mouth. It looked so bizarre, then so real. If you looked at it long enough your mind adjusted to the optical illusion and made it appear a correct face, right-side up.

"You try it," Taylor insisted.

We took turns hanging over the beds and making each other laugh. We did it at the same time, while the blood weighed down our heads and made us dizzy.

"You two better not still be awake!" Mrs. Tyler called out from somewhere in the house.

We quickly flipped back, and I dove under the covers. Taylor got up to shut out the light. She kept her door open just a little so that a shaft of light from the hall lay across her floor. I could hear a shower running from the bathroom in the master bedroom.

Taylor and I talked about school, about the other kids, about The Ones, and about Amber, who did finally come to school in new platform sneakers, not black but red.

Then the water shut off, and a few minutes later Mrs. Tyler appeared at the door. She wore a white terry cloth bathrobe, long to the floor. A white towel was turbaned on top of her head. She looked like a queen. (I silently noted to myself that I would have to add this to my list. I swore to myself that one day I would own a bathrobe like that.) She came into the room and sat at the end of Taylor's bed.

"Try and get a good night's sleep," she told Taylor. She patted Taylor's feet through the thick blankets.

"We will," Taylor answered.

Mrs. Tyler kissed her daughter on the top of her head and then stood up. She paused in the doorway, backlit by the hall light, creating a tall, graceful silhouette.

"Good night, Taylor," she called softly.

"Good night, Mommy," Taylor said.

"Good night, Gabby."

"Good night, Mrs. Tyler."

And she left. Her footsteps padded away from our door.

I was seized with a pang of jealousy that I had never felt so strongly before. It wasn't as much that Taylor said "Good night, Mommy" as what I had said: "Good night, Mrs. Tyler."

Had I ever said "Good night, Mommy" to anyone?

It reminded me of my dream, the one I had about Taylor's house. The mother's voice calling out but not to me. In my dream I had been crying, but now, awake, I could not.

I lay quiet, but I didn't fall asleep. Some time passed in the darkness. I heard Taylor crying softly.

"What's wrong?"

"Oh, I'm sorry. I thought you were sleeping," Taylor said.

"No, I'm awake. What's wrong?" I pushed myself up and crossed my legs.

"I miss my father," Taylor confessed. She remained lying down, staring up at the ceiling while she spoke. "I know I always say how happy I am that my mom is happy and about Richard and everything . . . but I miss my dad so much."

I tried to think of what I could say to comfort her. After all, I of all people should be able to understand.

"I know it's hard," I said.

"I always miss him at night. He used to tell me stories before I went to bed."

"My dad does that, too," I said. As I thought of it, I started feeling homesick.

Taylor wasn't really listening. It sounded like the first time she had thought these things. First time she said them out loud. They were meant more for her than for me.

"It's harder for me, I think," Taylor started slowly. "I mean, what happened to your mother . . . well, it happened so long ago. I still have to live with this all the time." Taylor sniffed. "Every time I leave my dad's apartment I feel terrible all over again. Every time."

Taylor cried softly, but I didn't try to say anything else. I lay back down in the bed and looked hard into the endless grayness where the ceiling would be if the light were on.

I felt so completely wronged, simply because there was nothing I could say to defend myself. There were no words to describe my pain, because I wasn't supposed to have any. What happened to my mother happened so long ago, it wasn't supposed to matter anymore.

Hadn't I spent my whole life proving that very point?

Chapter 15

Taylor had a tennis lesson first thing Saturday morning. I was grateful that Mrs. Tyler was dropping me off at my house early in order to get Taylor to the Field Club on time. I didn't want Taylor to see that I was upset. My sadness had turned to anger and grown during the night. I didn't know at who or for what, but I knew I couldn't hide it long.

We woke up, dressed in a hurry, ate on the run, and the next thing I knew I was saying "Thank you for having me" and waving good-bye from my front lawn. Taylor and her mom drove off down my driveway.

I could hear Ian inside playing electric jazz. He was plugged in. I saw Cleo's Volkswagen parked in front of the garage. So she had stayed over again.

Cleo used to leave very early in the morning, before she thought Ian and I were awake. Ian probably *was* sleeping, but I certainly was not. I used to hear Cleo's noisy car starting up before the sun. But they didn't bother hiding that anymore. My dad had never let that happen with anyone else.

I must have been standing still for a while, staring at nothing, before I felt how cold it was out there. I suddenly had this tremendous urge to tell Cleo what had happened. I wanted to tell her how my heart had clamped up last night when Taylor said her life was worse than mine. I wanted Cleo to explain my anger to me, to tell me I was justified in being so mad. I wanted something from Cleo. And though I wasn't sure what, I was certain she could give it to me; as certain as I was that I couldn't talk to my dad about it. It was all part of that stuff we never talk about, so we can pretend it never happened.

I opened the back door and was met by the warmth from the studio's space heater, which was humming loudly.

"Hi, sweetie," my dad said, still busy at his desk.

The extension arm of his clip-on lamp stretched as far as it could over his work space. There were no windows, since the studio was a sectioned-off part of the garage, which my dad had built when we first moved here, but an overhead light lit the whole room so he could work.

"Hi, Dad," I said. "Where's Cleo?"

I started past him toward the inner door to the house.

"She's not here. A friend of hers picked her up. They went to look at some fabric warehouse," he said. Then he looked up from the sketchbook he was drawing in. "Why?" he asked.

"Nothing," I said, but I couldn't believe the disappointment that was creeping up on me. I felt sick.

"Gabby?" My dad was looking at me now. He put down his piece of charcoal. He always made a sketch before he began work on his big paintings.

"What?" Anxiousness sounded in my voice, but my dad didn't notice it.

"I'm glad you're here, because I wanted to talk to you, anyway." He coughed. Not just a little. My dad is a real throat-clearer. But I am used to it. I know he's around when I hear it.

"What about?" I said. I wandered away from him, toward the easel.

Whatever this was, I didn't want to hear it. My dad never used the words I *want to talk to you*.

I stuck my fingers in the little mounds of drying oil paints. The outer shell of oil paint hardens, but underneath is a treasure of wet color. It oozes out from the sides or any little hole you make in it.

When I was little, my dad used to set up a little easel for me right beside his. He used an oversized sketch pad propped up inside an old clothing rack. He taped the pad to the sides with duct tape. I could paint while he painted, and I wasn't supposed to talk. But my paintings talked. Well, the fanned-out brush strokes that I made talked. They ran around the paper, chasing each other and getting into trouble. (Getting into trouble was a big explosion of oil paints all mixed together and swirled around till the paper almost ripped.)

Sometimes my dad took one of my paintings, framed it, and hung it in the house.

"Well, I've already tried talking to Ian." My dad cleared his throat again.

This must be something bad.

It's really the smell of my dad's studio that I love. And it always stays the same — turpentine, oil paint, even the woven, natural smell of a brand-new canvas. It was like I was born into this, so when I walk in and smell the studio, I know I am home.

"I'm expecting more from you, Gabby," my dad went on. "I'm hoping that . . ."

I turned away and walked toward a big painting my dad was working on. It was a scene from the farm just up the road. Two cows grazing in a flat field. Mostly the picture was the sky with huge, white clouds suspended in air.

"Gabby, it's about Cleo. I know how much you like her."

Oh, no. It is bad. I felt tears jerk into my eyes. There was a small pond that the two cows were going to drink from. The shadows of the clouds darkened the grass below.

"I wondered what you think of Cleo and me getting married. . . ."

"You are?" I whisked myself around. "You already told Ian? What did he say?"

"Not much," my dad told me.

"Well, I think that's a great idea, Dad," I said.

He looked relieved to be done talking. He picked up his charcoal and began working again. "You know your brother doesn't like change. That's all there is to that," he said.

But for some reason I thought there was more to "that" than that.

Chapter 16

After talking with my dad I plopped down on the couch to watch TV. When Cleo got back I could talk to her. Soon, I supposed, I could talk to her whenever I wanted.

Ian was still in his room practicing through his amplifier, loudly. He had his synthesizer going, too, with a fast, constant rhythm. Usually when Ian is playing too loud my dad goes and raps on his bedroom door and yells, "Keep it down!" But my dad was still out in the studio, and I guess his staying away had something to do with whatever Ian had said when my dad mentioned marriage. The bass on Ian's amplifier vibrated the walls.

Then it all stopped.

I was finally getting to watch (and hear) my show when Ian appeared in the doorway. He didn't say anything for the longest while. Then he spoke in this annoyed tone of voice, as if he had been trying to get my attention for hours.

"I hope you told him it was the worst idea he's ever

had." Ian glared at me. He didn't step out all the way into the living room.

"Huh?" came out before I figured out what he was talking about.

"I hope you weren't a wuss," Ian said.

"You're a wuss," I answered back.

There is a kind of language between my brother and me. We don't have to use many words, but we know what the other one means. Ian understood that I had said Dad getting married to Cleo was okay, and I knew Ian was saying he wanted me to stick with him. And oppose Dad.

I have to admit, for a moment I was torn. Ian had never asked me for anything, that I could remember. He didn't *need* me for anything, and yet, here he was. He needed me.

I flipped off the television.

"I like Cleo," I defended.

"So what?" he shot back. "You can like her all you want. She doesn't have to move in with us and ruin everything."

I hadn't even considered that she'd move in. I had just been so glad she wasn't leaving. Now I thought about it. I could watch how she did things. She could make me lunches for school. Maybe show me how to wear my hair. Ian wouldn't have to baby-sit me on the Saturdays when my dad had his first-weekend-of-the-month class.

I could fill up my list journal in no time.

"Ruin what?"

mother's regal tone of voice. "Oh, well, that's what rugs are for — to catch the spills. Tee-hee-hee."

I started to smile. "Hmmm."

Taylor must have heard my smile, because then she tried even harder. "Ha! Sure, Ma, that's what rugs are for! Wanna see what the couch is for?"

I had to laugh. "Got milk?"

Right away, Taylor came back with, "I looove the chocolate glaze!"

It felt good to laugh.

"Hurry, get a paper towel," I added, to see if Taylor remembered the spill on her leather couch.

She howled for what felt like a full minute. I couldn't help but to join in, and it felt good to laugh.

"Gabby?" Taylor's voice dropped. "I'm sorry about what I said the other night. About your mother. About my life being harder than yours. I didn't mean it," she said. "I was just feeling sorry for myself."

"You're the best friend I've ever had," Taylor told me then.

"Mine, too," I said.

"You're my YBF."

"Your what?"

"Your Best Friend," Taylor explained. "I used to have a sort-of best friend at my other school. Not like you, Gabby. But her older sister made that up. She used to sign her letters like that to her best friend — YBF. So we used it for a while."

"YBF," I said, trying it out. "I like it."

"I'll see you in school, YBF," Taylor said.

"Okay, YBF. Bye."

"Bye."

It was just beginning to rain when I hung up the phone. It drummed steadily, filling the river and soaking into the ground, all through that night.

Chapter 18

It was raining so hard the next morning. My brother's friend Paul had picked up Ian in his van and driven them to the high school. Paul was a couple of years older than Ian and played bass and keyboards. In Paul's presence, I was always certain to say something dumb, and not just my normal dumb, either. So I had hidden in my room till I was sure they were gone.

Cleo knocked on my bedroom door and called out, "Want me to drive you down the driveway? It's pouring."

I accepted Cleo's offer not only because I didn't want to get soaked, but also because waiting in my room so long, I was late. I hopped into the passenger side of Cleo's V.W. We waited at the end of the driveway. Our view of my bus stop and the farm next door was visible for a second, then pelted again with raindrops, as the windshield wipers flew back and forth.

"Why don't I just drive you to school?"

"Are you sure it's okay?" I asked. I didn't want to get out into that rain, but I wasn't one to ask for favors.

"Oh, once you're in the car it doesn't make any difference," Cleo said in a singsong voice. And we pulled out in the pouring rain.

For a while it was just the sound of the wipers: *swoosh, swoosh. Swoosh, swoosh.*

"So your dad talked to you the other day?" Cleo finally spoke.

"Yeah," I said. "He said you guys were thinking about getting married."

"That's what he said?" Cleo's voice squeaked.

Swoosh, swoosh. Squeak. Swoosh, swoosh.

"He told you we're thinking about getting married?" She said this a bit more calmly, but she was hitting the brakes too much and letting up on the clutch too quickly.

"I mean, he said you *were* getting married, and he asked me what I thought." I hoped that was better.

It seemed to be. Cleo switched right over to, "Your dad told me that you're happy about it." Cleo was back to normal. No beating around the bush. Open.

"Yeah. Aren't you?"

Cleo let out a sharp laugh. "Well, I would hope so."

We were in town. The rain kept the streets empty of people. Cars pulled in and out of stores and side streets. We stopped and started again. Then stopped completely. The one traffic light in New Paltz was red.

"But Ian doesn't agree with you, I take it," Cleo said again as soon as we were moving, past the old Elting Library, up the hill toward the newer sections of town. I thought that must have been hard for Cleo to say, but she didn't show it.

"Oh, Ian's a big jerk. Who cares about Ian?" I said, and I instantly regretted it. For two reasons. The first one was just a thought — the image of a lonely Ian no one cared about. The second reason was more immediate — Cleo didn't like what I said, and I could tell that right away.

"I care about Ian," Cleo said, making me feel worse. "He's had to adjust to living without a mother for all these years, and now the thought of some new woman living in his house must be hard."

He hasn't had to adjust to anything, I thought. Ian is just so used to being mean, he can't be anything else. What does Cleo know?

"No, really he's just stubborn," I stayed in my fair territory, but I softened my tone, just to sound nicer. She would see I was right.

"He may even feel like he's betraying her," Cleo said.

"Who?"

"Your mother," Cleo said. She turned left onto LeFevre Street. The middle school was built in what once was an apple orchard. There were still old, bent-over trees lining the way.

"No," I protested. "He doesn't even remember her. He never talks about that at all."

This conversation was getting very uncomfortable. Why was I feeling like the villain? It was Ian; he was the problem. Not me.

"Just because he doesn't talk about it, doesn't mean he isn't thinking about it. Missing her," Cleo said softly.

Now I was really angry. I couldn't miss my mother if I wanted to. And Ian didn't, either.

Though once a long time ago, when Ian and I were visiting our grandparents before Nana died and Grandpa got married again, we were alone and we were talking. Ian asked me if I remembered anything.

Did I remember that morning she died?

"What morning?" I asked.

"When we tried to wake her up?"

"How did we do that?"

"Do you remember when we went in the elevator?" he asked.

"We did?"

"Do you remember the doorman?"

"The what?"

Ian stopped talking then. But ever since, I've had my own memory of riding in an elevator with Ian. Everything is dark all around us, and then there is a bright light. It's so much like a memory — and I know it isn't real. My brother asked me some questions, and so I made up some pictures in my mind to go with it. Now it's stuck there in my brain, calling itself a memory even though it's not.

Cleo pulled up the brake and jiggled her stick shift. We were three cars behind the drop-off to the New Paltz middle school. Two apple trees away.

I saw Lynette get out of her truck just ahead. She had her knapsack and a Grand Union grocery bag in her hands.

Oh, crud! I suddenly remembered that I was supposed to bring the heavy cream for my group's final home economics project. My project group was Amber, Lynette, and me.

Of course, Amber will have her ingredient. Look, even Lynette remembered. Oh, damn, I thought. I closed my eyes against the worry, against facing the home ec. teacher and Amber, who would be furious if I ruined the rice pudding.

"What's the matter?" Cleo asked.

If Cleo were my mother she would run to the Grand Union right away, as soon as I mentioned that I had forgotten something. She wouldn't think twice. And she'd get me what I needed and bring it to the office, labeled with my name.

But I couldn't ask. She might not be able to go, and then Cleo would be uncomfortable having to tell me she couldn't do it. Or worse: She'd say no, and I'd have to feel terrible that I had asked and she said no.

No, I couldn't even imagine asking.

But wouldn't it be nice if I asked and she had smiled and said, "Yes, of course. I'll get you whatever you need."

"So are you getting married to my dad or not?" I asked as I opened the car door to get out. As if I cared anymore.

"Yes. Yes, I am," Cleo said firmly.

I was so glad. Soon, real soon, I'd be able to ask for heavy cream, if I ever forgot to bring it again.

Chapter 19

"I can't believe it," Amber was saying. She put her hands up to her head and rocked it back and forth as if she'd just learned that someone had dumped nuclear waste into the town's water supply.

"It's not that big a deal," I said.

Lynette, Amber, and I were in kitchen unit number seven, the one in the far corner by the window, where the rain outside hit steadily against the panes. Each kitchen unit had a stove, a sink, and a wood-block table. There was only one refrigerator for everyone, and that was in the main kitchen area. Mrs. Drummond, the home ec. teacher, was in kitchen unit number three helping Peter, Kevin, and Booby with their baked Alaska. (That's his name — Booby, as in booby prize. His real name is Abe.) From the sound of things, the baked Alaska wasn't going well.

"By the time she gets to us, she'll be in a really bad mood," Amber wailed. "How could you forget one little container of cream?"

I turned to look at Amber with my don't-start-with-me look, but Lynette was suddenly in the way.

"It will be all right." Lynette recited, "Three tablespoons of butter and seven-eighths of a cup of milk."

Amber paid no attention. As far as she was concerned, Lynette could be singing a nursery rhyme. Peter and Booby were flicking egg whites all over each other while Kevin was getting ready to put their baked Alaska in the oven. Mrs. Drummond left them and headed over to unit number five. There, everything seemed to be under control. Mrs. Drummond was smiling again.

"Three tablespoons of butter and seven-eighths of a cup of milk," Lynette said again.

We had already started to cook the Minute Rice and milk and added the raisins before I had the heart to tell my group about the missing cream.

"I brought the rice," Amber ranted. "*And* I brought the eggs!"

Amber was stirring the mixture of vanilla, sugar, and eggs sans heavy cream. "This is for our final grade."

"Your grade for sixth-grade rice pudding should not really be the most crucial moment in your life," I said. Still, I felt terrible, and I had already checked everyone else's supplies. No one had heavy cream.

We could hear Mrs. Drummond praising unit five on their strawberry shortcake.

"Three tablespoons of butter and seven-eighths of a cup of milk," Lynette said.

"Will you stop saying that!" Amber turned to Lynette.

"What?" I said, trying to remember what I had just heard but hadn't listened to. "What did she say?"

"Something about butter," Amber said curtly.

"Three tablespoons of butter and seven-eighths of a cup of milk is the same as one cup of heavy cream," Lynette repeated.

Amber raised the heat on the rice and milk. It bubbled slowly in loud plops. "Maybe it will just get thicker if I boil it. Get ready to add the egg stuff. Lynette, get those little saucers ready."

"Let's try what Lynette says," I said suddenly.

The bottom of the milk and rice was starting to stick to the pan. A burning smell rose from the stove.

"Oh, no," Amber said and threw the pan off the burner. It sizzled. "What does Lynette know!? She was hit by a truck."

I was stricken, but Lynette didn't seem bothered by the comment at all.

"Three tablespoons of butter and seven-eighths of a cup of milk," she said.

"Well, I'm going to try it," I told Amber.

We already had the milk. I had to sneak over to borrow butter from Peter's group while Mrs. Drummond was tasting group six's ladyfingers.

When I asked, Peter threw a stick of soft butter at me, and somehow I caught it before the butter hit the floor and smushed.

"Good catch," Peter said.

"Thanks," I called over my shoulder as I hurried back to my unit.

Amber was so nearly comatose with worry that Lynette and I had to save the rice pudding by ourselves. We slipped the pan in the oven just as Mrs. Drummond came over and peaked into the viewing window. The rice pudding sat like miniature boats in a shallow pond. When she asked us how everything went we told the truth.

"Oh, that is clever. A good cook always knows her substitutes." She even clapped. "Amber, that must have been your idea. Am I right?"

No one said anything. Lynette didn't, so Amber sure didn't. But Amber was biting her lip and looking worried. I kind of liked Amber then, like maybe she had a conscience but not enough of one to credit Lynette for her idea.

Mrs. Drummond announced our rice pudding earned us all an A+, and she walked away.

Amber finally spoke. "Thanks, Lynette." She twisted a pot holder in her hands and looked down at the floor.

Just as Lynette was going to say something, the bell rang to end the period. We finished up the dishes and got ready to leave. The rice pudding was safely in the refrigerator. I placed the last mixing bowl on the drying rack. Amber thanked Lynette again and left quickly. She still looked pretty shook up.

"Amber didn't mean what she said," I told Lynette, but I didn't want to look right at her. "About you not knowing anything." I worked diligently on wiping the counter, but I could feel Lynette's attention focus behind me.

"I wasn't hit by a truck, you know," Lynette said.

"What?" I kept rubbing around in one spot.

"I was in an incubator right after I was born, and the doctor forgot to turn on the air for a couple of seconds," Lynette said. "I know the story about the truck, but that's all it is — a story." She was talking fast now.

I looked around to see if anyone was listening to this. Only Mrs. Drummond was still in the room, at her desk, bent over in concentration. The second bell was about to ring.

"That's the truth." Lynette seemed desperate.

"Oh, well that's okay," I said, quickly grabbing my knapsack. "We better get going."

"I thought you'd understand. I thought you'd want to know the truth," Lynette said. Her face held a puzzled look.

"I'm sorry but . . . the bell's gonna ring." I started to leave. I didn't think I wanted to hear any more.

Chapter 20

It was the start of Thanksgiving vacation. Taylor was going to spend it at her dad's. I couldn't help being a little glad to hear the sadness in her voice when Taylor told me. I was going to miss her, too, and it's so much better to miss someone who's also missing you. We weren't going to be able to talk on the phone for almost a week.

I had no idea what my family was doing for Thanksgiving. When Taylor asked me, I told her we always had Thanksgiving at home. But when I thought about it, with Cleo in the picture, I really wasn't sure.

No one was home when I got off the bus. There was a note from my dad that he had to go to the college for a department meeting. I didn't know where Ian was. I found myself more than half wanting and half expecting Cleo to be home.

As far as I was concerned, Cleo was totally moved in. She had moved the colander in the kitchen from the dish cabinet to the pot cabinet, and the can opener from the place-mat drawer to the wooden-spoon drawer. She never spent more than one night back at her place anymore.

My dad's bathroom was more filled with her things than his own. This, I loved. When Cleo wasn't around I liked to poke around and touch her stuff. She had a pink razor and tampons, lip gloss and nail-polish remover, a wooden hairbrush and ladies' deodorant. And a bottle of something called Woolite under the sink. I was considering looking through Cleo's stuff again, since she wasn't home, maybe trying out her razor on my legs, in a spot no one would see.

But first, I'd get myself something to eat in the kitchen. I sat at the table with a box of Goldfish crackers and some juice. I stared out the window for a while and listened for the sound of a car over the gravel driveway; Cleo's car or my dad's car.

That's when I felt it.

I felt like I was peeing in my pants. In fact, that's what I first thought — I thought I was peeing in my pants, so I just got up and went to the bathroom. I leaned way over as I sat down, so I saw two little drops of red fall into the toilet.

This was it. *Oh, my God.*

This was it.

It. I wanted to scream for someone.

But no one was home. For the first half an hour I ran around the house, excited and nervous. I calmed down long enough to get out my journal — Book Two — and

was on the knob, but she didn't open it. I was glad for the distance between the bed (me) and the door (her).

"When you and my dad get married . . . ," I began, "am I supposed to . . . ? Will you . . . ? Should I . . . ? Can I call you Mom?"

There are single moments in my life that take longer than any others. Seconds that linger and suck all the air out of me, like I'm inside a bell jar. This was one of them. Cleo's hesitation was one horrible second too long. Her face was frozen, her hand was still on the doorknob. Not completely in, but nearly heading out.

"Is that what you want?" Cleo asked me, still stopped by the door.

But what I wanted was so much more than that. And it seemed on this very day, as I became a "woman," my oldest wish was going to be lost to me forever. For me it was too late. Too late to have a mom.

"No, I wouldn't want that. I was just asking what you thought," I said.

When I looked out the kitchen window later that afternoon, I noticed the river had risen. Trees that had stood low on the banks now looked as though they were floating. Their branches made trails in the flowing water.

Chapter 21

"It's tonight? Not tonight," I complained.

"I told you." My dad looked at me. "Didn't I?"

No, he definitely hadn't told me the Faculty Show was that night. Or maybe I knew but I forgot. Either way, I had just started my Thanksgiving vacation, I had just gotten my very first menstrual period, so I should have been resting, and besides, it was cold and rainy out.

"Well, if you don't want to go . . ." My dad was putting on a tie. "I suppose you're old enough to stay home alone."

"In fact, you're a woman now." My dad smiled at me. So Cleo had told him. And she had left to get changed at her house, right away. I didn't even hear her leaving. But I did find the necessary item left discreetly on my bed.

"I hate wearing a tie." My dad tugged at his shirt collar.

We were all hanging out in my dad's bathroom. Ian was shaving (although I thought that was a waste of shaving cream and I told him so). My dad pulled off his tie and started all over again.

I had this funny thought, while we were all jammed into the bathroom. I was sitting on the edge of the bathtub. I remembered when Ian and I used to take baths together, and if my dad was shaving he would put shaving cream on our faces and we would shave each other's cheeks using a toothbrush. I *so* definitely remember when Ian refused to take a bath with me anymore. All of a sudden I was ashamed, and I was embarrassed for all the times I *hadn't* been ashamed. It was a long time ago, but I could feel that feeling right then like it was just the day before. Embarrassed.

"All right, all right. I'll go," I said, standing up quickly.

"Good, because Cleo's going to meet us there," my dad said. "By the way, Cleo said she'd stop at the drugstore for you," he added, not quite looking at me. Ian kept his concentration on his careful shaving.

Embarrassed. For all of us.

I think in the end I just didn't want to be home alone on this most important day of my life. Maybe I'd have my first taste of wine from one of those little plastic cups, and then I'd have two important things to write about in my journal for one day.

I completely forgot that Mrs. Tyler had said she wanted to go to this opening until we got there — until we walked in and I saw her standing next to some eventaller-than-she-is man in a blue blazer. *Richard Tyler,* I thought. *Wait till I tell Taylor I saw him.*

I headed in the opposite direction, away from the Tylers. I wasn't in the mood for Mrs. Tyler. Not tonight. My dad headed right for the metal folding table and took a glass of wine from the triangle formation of mini plastic cups. I headed for an empty corner of the room. Ian sort of drifted along with me.

The room was set up with three freestanding walls on which the smaller paintings and photographs were hung — watercolor paintings, collages, black-and-white portraits. One artist displayed tiny clay boxes with sticks inside. I thought they looked like something I could have made in kindergarten.

The larger oil paintings were hung on the four permanent walls of the room. I saw my dad's cows, clouds, and river views all around me. His paintings were among the biggest. They were, I thought, by far the best.

I recognized some of the other art professors milling around the room, also with little cups of wine in their hands. Someone always smoked cigarettes at these things even though they weren't allowed to. I was getting a headache and a little menstrual cramp, I thought.

"How long is this going to last?" Ian said to me.

"I don't know. But Dad isn't going to want to stay long." I sat down on the floor, tightly crossed my legs, and leaned my back against a beam.

"He might want to stay this time," Ian said. "Cleo might make him."

I didn't want to talk about Cleo. I didn't want to think of how stupid I must have sounded asking Cleo if I could call her Mom. The key to surviving embarrassing moments is to not think about them. Then Dad spotted us. He hurried over and stood with me and Ian in the corner by my beam.

"I hate these things," he said. He yanked at his tie to loosen it, so now it hung cockeyed, caught on the button of his dress shirt.

"What things?" Ian asked. "Openings? Or your tie?"

"Both," he answered with no sense of humor whatsoever. "When is Cleo going to get here? So we can leave."

I looked over at Ian with an I-told-you-so eyebrow lift.

"Oh, there she is," he said suddenly. Cleo had come in. She walked right by Mr. and Mrs. Tyler. She looked beautiful. She was wearing a short black dress and cowboy boots. She looked cool and elegant at the same time. I saw Mrs. Tyler pull Mr. Tyler off toward a painting on the other side of the room.

Cleo was holding something in her hands, but I couldn't see what it was. She looked around the room, her eyes scanning. She caught sight of us. A big smile drew across her face and she headed over.

"Why are you guys all hiding here?" she said with a laugh. "Larry, go mingle. I heard people looking for you. The department head is here."

"That's exactly why I'm leaving in five minutes. I made my appearance. I'll get you a drink," my dad said. "Then we'll go."

He headed back to the metal folding table. Ian trailed right behind him.

"Gabby," Cleo said right away before I could follow them. "I wanted to give you something. To commemorate this evening for you."

She was holding out a gift, wrapped in natural paper with brown twine. I took it. I flipped it over in my hands and looked at it. It was small, hard, and square. Like a box of . . . sanitary pads.

"It's not that," she said and let go a laugh as if she read my thoughts. "I did stop at the pharmacy, but that box is in my car. This is a gift. Really. That's why I left so quickly. I wanted to get to this special store before it closed."

Oh.

She nodded for me to open it. Slowly I unwrapped the paper. Underneath was a blank book, like the one I used to write down my dreams and the one I compiled my list in and the one I used for a journal. Only this one was special. It had a red cover made of velvety paper with tiny, dried flowers pressed right into it. It was tied shut with a fat red ribbon. It was beautiful.

"Open it," she urged.

I pulled open the ribbon and lifted the front cover. There was an inscription inside, written in Cleo's swirly lettering.

For your most private thoughts, for your dreams
For your wishes, and hopes, and new beginnings on this special day
To Gabby with love,

Your Mom-to-be,

Cleo

I felt so large right then. I felt like I took up the whole room. I was too big, too old. I was almost as tall as Cleo.

I felt huge. I felt so dumb. Cleo was only eighteen years older than Ian. Only twenty-one years older than me.

Can I call you Mom? Had I really said that? What had I been thinking?

"I didn't really mean . . . ," I stammered.

"I know," she stopped me. "I won't . . . I can't even try to guess how it feels not having a mom. I only hope I can be a part of your life, a good part, at least. It's all new and we're both learning."

As large and clumsy as I felt in that room, exposed by the bright fluorescent lights and betrayed by my own changing body, I wanted what Cleo was offering. I still wanted it. I had always wanted it.

"If you don't want to . . . ," I said, my voice shaking.

Cleo stopped me. "We can be for each other, Gabby, whatever we can be."

My dad and Ian came back. My dad had all our coats draped over his arm.

"No wine, Larry?" Cleo looked at my dad. "I just got here."

"I really hate these things," my dad said, as if that was an explanation.

"Larry . . . ," Cleo began, but then she took her coat from my dad. "Oh, you artist types," she said.

I clutched my book to my chest. Ian was wrong. Cleo wasn't going to ruin us. Just the opposite. This was going to be better than great.

On our way out we bumped into Mrs. and Mr. Tyler. *I can do this,* I convinced myself. *I watch TV.*

105

"Dad, this is Taylor's mother, Mrs. Tyler," I introduced her to my dad.

So far, so good.

They said their hellos, then Mr. Tyler stuck out his hand.

"Richard Tyler," he said, unprompted.

My dad shook his hand, too.

"Your paintings are wonderful," Mrs. Tyler said. "I do a little interior design. Maybe we could work together sometime."

I cringed. Mrs. Tyler couldn't have said a worse thing to my dad if she had tried. (Unless she was going to ask my dad if he had any paintings with maybe just a touch more mountain to pick up the brown tones in her client's beige walls.)

"This is my brother, Ian," I said quickly, before my dad had time to respond.

Both Mr. and Mrs. Tyler shook Ian's hand.

"And this is Cleo Bloom," I said. "Just Cleo. Not my mom. Just Cleo."

Cleo took my hand behind her back and squeezed it; at the same time, she reached out with her other hand and said hello to Taylor's mom and Richard.

"Nice to meet you," Mrs. Tyler said. Mrs. Tyler had this confused look on her face, like "So, then, who are you?" But none of us offered any more information.

"Gabby has talked a lot about your daughter, Taylor," Cleo said. "I can't wait to meet her."

"Oh," Mrs. Tyler said. "Oh, yes. Well . . . of course."

"Bye," I said. I waved and Cleo and I walked out to the car, still side by side. My dad just wanted out of there. He and Ian led the way.

"That was Mrs. Tyler?" Ian said when we got out into the parking lot. "And your friend is Taylor? Taylor Tyler? You're kidding, right?" Ian laughed. "That's her name? Taylor Tyler?"

I was too content to correct him or to let him get to me this time.

It had stopped raining. By the time we got home there were at least two inches of snow on the ground.

Chapter 22

It snowed again Wednesday, and by Thanksgiving we
had half a foot. The river disappeared under the never-
ending whiteness. You couldn't tell the frozen water
from the frozen ground. Animal footprints led from one
side of the river straight across to the other. Large, brown
branches trapped and sticking out of the ice were the
only hint that what lay underneath was not always solid.
Everywhere was white.

"We have to leave in ten minutes," Cleo was saying.
She had been pacing around the house for the last hour.
I had never seen her so nervous before. We were going to
Long Island, to her parents' house for Thanksgiving din-
ner. So that's what we were doing for Thanksgiving. I'd
have to tell Taylor.

"Cleo, it's not going to take us three hours to get
there," my dad told her.

"Three hours!" I called out.

I hated sitting in the car for that long. I was in my
room, fighting with a pair of tights. Then my tights were

fighting my skirt. With every step I took, my skirt crawled higher up my legs and the crotch of my tights sank lower. I changed into my overalls and a T-shirt and came out into the living room.

"I thought you said it was less than two hours to Long Island," I complained to anyone who would listen.

"You'll live," Ian said, looking at me. He was sitting on the couch again, playing his guitar. Ian never spoke much to me before, but with Cleo around, he spoke even less. Two or three words, tops.

Cleo was dressed up in a long skirt and big earrings. She looked me over but didn't say anything. Ian carefully put his guitar in its case and leaned it against the wall. My dad jingled his keys. We were ready.

"How long is this drive, really?" I asked as we all walked through the studio out to the garage.

No one answered me.

I was carsick before we were out of the Wallkill Valley. I sat by the window and watched the telephone poles fly by. I felt worse. I tried looking straight out between my dad's seat and Cleo's. Before this new family arrangement, Ian would be in front and I could sit in the center of the back seat, looking out past the dashboard. Now I could only stare straight at the back of the front seat. I was feeling motion sick. I started singing to myself to keep my mind off my stomach.

"Dad, tell her *stop*." Four words from Ian.

"What?" I said. "I'm not doing anything." I kept singing softly.

"Then be quiet." Ian didn't bother to look at me while he complained about me.

When we were younger, if we were fighting in the car my dad would just reach his hand back like he was trying to hit us and swing around at anything. He would growl and grunt, and we'd all wind up laughing. If Ian and I got into a really bad fight he would make us stare at each other without smiling for sixty seconds. (For this purpose my dad kept a little egg timer in the glove compartment.) Ian or I or both of us would crack up before the minute was up and forget what we had been fighting about.

"Dad, make her be quiet," Ian said. "I can't stand listening to her."

"Just knock it off back there," my dad shouted without taking his eyes off the road. "There's a lot of traffic."

Cleo was breathing carefully in and out. "I told you we should have left more time for traffic. My father says I'm always late. It's his big joke."

"Cleo, we'll be fine," my dad said.

I started singing again.

"You sound terrible. Will you cut it out?" Still Ian didn't look at me. He was turned to the world rushing past his window.

"You sing off-key," Ian said to his window. He meant it for me.

"I do not," I defended myself, as I had to, but what I thinking was that Ian *would* know something like that. Wouldn't he?

My dad made his loud hiss from between his teeth. That's when you knew he was really mad. Cleo sighed. I stopped singing. Not because of Ian telling me to stop, or the hiss, or the sigh. But because Ian said I sang off-key.

I did? I didn't inherit anything musical? Figures. I probably inherited carsickness, but even that I couldn't say for sure.

I took out my Game Boy, flipped it on, and turned off the sound. We pulled into the Blooms' driveway ninety minutes later.

Chapter 23

We were on Long Island. Or in Long Island, I'm not sure
which is correct. The Blooms had a house just like the
house next to them and the house next to that. A single-
story, half-brick and half-wood home with a flat driveway
and low, neatly trimmed evergreen bushes by the entrance.

As I got out of the car, I could see through the big
window in the front of the house. Mrs. Bloom was walking by with a plate in her hands. She put it down on a
table, I supposed, because I couldn't see what was below
the window. Mr. Bloom was sitting in a chair near where
the plate must have gone. Mrs. Bloom leaned over to Mr.
Bloom and kissed her husband on the head. It was one of
the most loving things I had ever seen. I liked these
people, before I even ran ahead on their brick walkway
and rang their doorbell.

"You must be Gabby!" Mrs. Bloom said as she opened
the door. Behind her I could see Mr. Bloom rising from
his chair.

I nodded. Cleo came up behind me, followed by my
dad and Ian.

"Hello!" Cleo sang out.

"Cleo!"

Then her father was at the door. "Cleo, my baby! I'm so glad you're here. I was getting worried."

"Sorry we're late, Daddy," Cleo said. "Just the usual me, right?"

"I didn't say you were late, Cleo," her father said. "I said I'm glad you're here."

"You're not late at all, darling," Mrs. Bloom said to Cleo, kissing her on the cheek. "Pay no attention to your father."

Cleo's parents didn't wait a second. They hugged and kissed each one of us. When Mr. Bloom bent down to hug me, I could see he had a little pierced earring.

Once inside the house, I could see the table where the plate had been set. Besides that one dish I had seen through the window, there was more food. There were crackers and cheese, and vegetables all cut up with dip. There was a small bowl of some brown stuff and more crackers next to that, and a bowl of M&M's. For a quick second I thought maybe this was dinner. Then I glanced into the dining room and saw a fully set table — woven tablecloth, candles, big ceramic dishes and bowls.

Mr. Bloom asked everyone what they wanted to drink right away. He started with Ian, which I think Ian liked. These were such friendly people, they didn't notice how crabby we were, and before you knew it everyone was as happy as they were.

Cleo asked her mother if she could help in the

kitchen, something I had seen before, a woman thing to do. Ian and my dad and Cleo's dad all sat around and dipped crackers into the dips. I sat with them. The brown stuff, I learned, was chopped liver and was the most delicious thing in the world. I ate most of it. Mr. Bloom was talking about the New York Giants, and I noticed my dad was really trying to keep up his end of the conversation, even though he doesn't follow sports that much and he never watches football.

I guess he was trying so hard for Cleo. To show Cleo, or her parents, to show himself maybe, that he could do it. When the topic went from football to artificial turf and then changed to gardening, he did pretty good. My dad loves his garden.

After a while I wandered into the kitchen. I was, after all, a woman now.

"So you want me to tell you what I think of him?" I heard Mrs. Bloom whisper. She was stirring something on the stove. From where I was, it smelled like gravy. Cleo stood beside her, pouring some white liquid stuff into the pan.

"Not really, Mom," Cleo was saying.

Cleo was so different here. She was less open.

"Well, he's adorable." Mrs. Bloom didn't seem to notice how *closed* Cleo was being.

"He is cute, isn't he?" Cleo looked over to her mom. "But I told you about —" Then Cleo saw me standing in the doorway.

"I bet Dad is going on about the New York Giants again." Cleo started toward me as if she were going to run right out into the living room and stop that conversation immediately.

"Oh, stop, Cleo," Mrs. Bloom said. She teasingly hit Cleo in the arm with her dishrag. "They'll be fine. All men like to talk about football."

"No, they don't, Mom," Cleo said. "And you know Dad never notices when the person he's talking to has absolutely no interest in what he's saying at all."

"They're not talking about football anymore," I said, but so quietly that neither of them heard me. Something was going on between them I couldn't understand. A tension was building and it made me uncomfortable. I wanted it broken.

"You're doing your thing," Mrs. Bloom said, more serious than she had been before. "You can't take care of everyone, Cleopatra."

"Cleopatra?" I butted in, this time a little louder.

"Oh, yes." Cleo turned to me like she just noticed I was there. "I never told you?"

Mrs. Bloom lifted the gravy pan and began pouring it through a strainer into a large bowl set up in the sink.

"Oh, here we go with 'Why did my parents name me that horrible, strange name,'" Mrs. Bloom chanted.

"My parents were hippies." Cleo stepped back into the kitchen. She picked a piece of turkey off the bone and popped it into her mouth.

"They had me during the Summer of Love," Cleo explained. "They were into that Indian-peace-feminist-freedom thing."

So far, tension still unbroken.

"Cleopatra wasn't an Indian," I said. I wanted them to keep talking. "Not American Indian. Not India Indian."

"No, but it sounded better than Indira Gandhi Bloom," Cleo said.

"Now, come to think of it," Mrs. Bloom said, as she put down the pan, "that sounds pretty good. Or maybe we should have named you Susan B. Anthony Bloom or Golda Meir Bloom." She giggled.

"Oooh, I got one," Cleo broke in. "How 'bout Amelia Bloomer Bloom!"

They both started laughing. Mrs. Bloom grabbed the corner of the butcher-block table, as if Cleo's jokes were just knocking her off her feet. Cleo kept going, making her mother laugh until they fell into each other's arms. Whatever tension had been there rose away and was lost, like the heat from the oven. They hadn't been scared of it in the first place. They didn't need any help; they'd had each other all along.

It was time for dinner.

"So, Cleo tells us you just had a show of your art-work?" Mr. Bloom said. He had finished cutting the turkey and was laying slices on everyone's plates as they were passed up to him.

"Well, yes." My dad looked uncomfortable, like he had just put a tie on again. I wished they'd stick to tomato plants and mulching, so my dad would look better. I saw Cleo give her father the warning eye but he wasn't looking when she did it.

"What kind of painting do you do?" Mr. Bloom asked.

"Landscapes, mostly," my dad said.

"We would have come up for the opening," Mrs. Bloom added. "If Cleo had told us about it."

"Mom-my," Cleo began, but my dad interrupted. "You didn't miss anything," he told them.

"Oh, you artist types," Mrs. Bloom chided kindly. I knew I had heard that expression before.

I sat and listened and ate everything before me. My dad seemed okay with all the questions, so Cleo stopped hissing from across the table. Cleo's parents turned from one person to the next. They asked Ian about his music and his teachers and his wonderful talent. Ian was particularly talkative. I think he liked the other Blooms more than he liked Cleo these days. Then they turned to me.

"So, Gabby," Mrs. Bloom said, "how are you doing in school?"

I said, "Fine."

"What is your favorite subject?" Mr. Bloom asked. I know that sounds like the dumbest question on earth, but I couldn't help liking him. All through dinner he kept offering me more of whatever I seemed to like. He had filled my glass of soda twice already. My dad never brought soda.

"Music," I answered.

I heard Ian choke on his stuffing.

"Oh, another musician," Mrs. Bloom said cheerfully. "Do you play an instrument, too?"

I looked Mrs. Bloom right in the eye and said, "No, I sing."

"How lovely," Mrs. Bloom said. "Anyone want any more stuffing?"

No one mentioned the upcoming Bloom/Weiss marriage until dinner was being cleared and coffee was perking. Ian, my dad, and Mr. Bloom went into the other room to look at Mr. Bloom's collection of shot glasses. He had a funny vacation anecdote for each one.

I didn't really love clearing the table and scraping the leftover food into the garbage. But I couldn't complain. I liked it enough being around Mrs. Bloom, and she didn't seem to mind all that work one bit. In fact, she was only worried if everyone had had enough to eat.

"Do you think your Larry wanted more turkey?" Mrs. Bloom asked Cleo. "He hardly ate."

"Now you're doing your thing, Mom," Cleo said.

I thought for a second they were going to go at it again, but Mrs. Bloom just laughed.

"Okay, fair enough," she said. "So when's the wedding? Do you have a date?"

"We're not doing that whole, big, wedding thing," Cleo told her mom. She slipped the last dish into the dishwasher and flipped up the door.

"Oh, why not?" Mrs. Bloom's voice went up like a little girl's. "You know you always wanted that. When we lived on that commune and we all had to wear plain coveralls, everything simple, remember? You used to say when you grew up you were going to be the most beautiful bride in the longest, most-satiny dress with pearl beads, pink ribbons, and lace."

"Remember that, Cleo?" Mrs. Bloom's voice smiled. She turned off the tap as if she were listening to her own memory. The way she looked into space, I could almost see Cleo's wedding dress.

"I remember." Cleo grinned. "And remember when you had to get a ladder and take me down from that giant Buddha statue because I climbed up there to paint his face?" she went on.

Mrs. Bloom remembered. "You said he looked sad. You know, as much as you said you'd rather live with the Brady Bunch, you loved it there," she told her daughter. "You were such a free little thing."

My family never did this; the back and forth with memories they had and tried to get the other person to remember. It was like we never existed before the right here and now. The Blooms had stories, and stories about those stories, that made them real, made them exist.

"Well, maybe a few pink ribbons and a little lace, then," Cleo said quietly. She leaned against the counter. "Maybe a couple of pearls."

That's when Mrs. Bloom got excited and went on and on. She had a friend whose brother was a big caterer.

"You only get married once," Mrs. Bloom said.

But that's when I lost interest and decided to slip out of the kitchen and go look at shot glasses.

Cleo must have looked to see that I was gone, because there was a long pause before she answered her mother.

"Remember, it's not Larry's first wedding, Mom," I heard Cleo say, but I was already hurrying to the living room, more interested in seeing what Ian had gotten.

The shot glasses were already put away. Mr. Bloom was showing Ian and my dad pictures of their recent trip to Israel. Ian held a small, foreign-looking string instrument in his hands. Judging from the wrapping paper on the table, the instrument had been a gift for Ian.

"Oh, here, I have something for you, too, Gabby," Mr. Bloom said when he saw me come into the den.

"I hope it's not too babyish." He handed me a train of four tiny, wooden camels, strung together by a miniature chain.

"I love it." I said as I breathed in.

I held my gift all the way back home in the car. I looked down into their little carved faces. I saw their expressions. They were a family, from big to small, connected from one end to the other. I almost fell asleep holding them in my lap. Ian had his present in his hands, too. He even let me listen to his Walkman. I was going to like this family.

I put the volume up on the Walkman, so I could barely even hear my dad and Cleo having a "discussion" about the wedding all the way home.

Chapter 24

I wanted to call Taylor as soon as I got up the next morning. She had said she'd be home by Thursday night, because she was going to have a second Thanksgiving with
her mom and Richard on Friday.

It had been a whole week and I hadn't told her my big
news yet — that I had gotten my first period. (Although
it was gone two days after that, almost as suddenly as it
had appeared.) And I hadn't even told her about Cleo yet,
let alone that my dad was getting married. Maybe it
hadn't really sunk in until Thanksgiving and all that
wedding talk.

I really needed to make this phone call.

I tiptoed out of bed. I didn't notice anything unusual
in the kitchen or anywhere else around the house. Except
that it was quiet. The windows were frosted with cold
condensation. The wood floor was freezing under my
bare feet. I looked at the clock — seven forty-five. Too
early to call Taylor. Mrs. Tyler looked like someone who
cared about her beauty sleep. She would definitely care if
I did something rude and called too early.

I'd just wait awhile.

By five past eight I was getting antsy. Where was Cleo? Ian was known to sleep through the whole morning. But my dad was an early riser. He got up with the first light, checked everything in the house, made his coffee, and was out in the studio working by seven. This morning I seemed to be the first one up. I decided I would eat something, then go look for someone. While I was contemplating the breakfast cereals in the pantry, I turned around to see my dad.

"You look terrible," I said.

"I didn't sleep much." He walked over to the sink to start the coffee. He opened three cabinets before he found the filters.

He really did look terrible. He filled the coffeepot with water.

"Dad, can I call Taylor?" I started. "Is it too early still? What would —" I didn't get to finish.

"Sure, sweetie." He walked out of the room. He forgot to plug in the coffee machine.

When Cleo was around so much in the beginning it felt weird. And then after a while it didn't anymore. But it's funny how things can fall right back to the way they were — so quiet, with Dad and Ian and me going about our business, not talking much. It was a long while before I even noticed.

"Cleo's still sleeping?" I asked, pressing my Rice Krispies into the milk.

My dad had wandered back into the kitchen. He

plugged in the coffee machine. The water starting steaming right away.

"Cleo's not going to be around anymore," he said. He stood watching the hot water drop into the glass coffee-pot.

My spoon stopped halfway to my mouth. That's when Ian walked in. He didn't look so good, either, but he never does.

"Cleo's gone?" Ian said.

"She left last night," Dad told us both. "It's all for the best. She wasn't ready to get married."

Cleo was gone?

"Is she coming back?" I asked. I pushed my bowl as far away as I could reach.

"No, as soon as she can get a flight she's going to her sister's in Colorado. Yeah, it's Colorado, I think."

The coffee was apparently ready enough, and my dad poured some into his mug as the rest of it dripped down onto the burner and spattered.

"She's coming back to say good-bye," I told my dad.

My dad turned to me. His eyes were puffy and his hair was uncombed. Something about him was so unfamiliar it made me feel unsafe, like the time I reached for my dad's hand at the gallery so long ago, a hand that turned out not to be his hand. I felt lost again.

"No, sweetie. I don't think so," he said. Then he spoke out loud, as if for someone's benefit, though not mine. "I tried to get her to change her mind," he said. "I tried till two in the morning."

"You're lying!" I screamed.

Then I cried. I don't remember for how long. I ran into my room and flung myself on my bed. I cried such sobs that my body hurt. My nose ran freely. I couldn't even think what it was I was crying about. My body was crying, my eyes were crying, my nose was crying. It didn't matter what I thought anymore. Crying had taken over and when it was done it left me like an empty rag doll.

My dad didn't know what to do with me. He sat on my bed for a while, and then he went away. He came back with some tea. Then he left again.

Taylor called me, but I couldn't talk.

Finally, after an hour or so, I got up and walked out of my room. I went straight down the hall to my dad's room. All of Cleo's stuff was gone. Her books by the bed, even her little reading light. The piece of Brazilian lace she had put on the bureau was gone, as well as the bottle of hand lotion that had been on top. She had two little mirrored boxes she kept her jewelry in. They were both gone.

I went into the bathroom. Her hairbrush and toothbrush were gone. Her Tom's Natural Toothpaste was gone. Her razor, her women's shave cream, even the Woolite was gone. Then I remembered the antique cigar box that Cleo used to hold Q-tips and cotton balls in the linen closet. I walked out into the hall and opened the closet. It was gone, too.

She had been so utterly thorough, I thought.

It was like she didn't want anyone to know she had ever been here. Ever.

I suddenly ran back to my room. I flung open my door and headed straight for my night table. Under the hanging piece of material I had my three notebooks and by my bed a fourth, the one Cleo had given me. Slowly I lifted that one into my hands. The ribbon was undone, although I was sure I always retied it whenever I looked at it. I hadn't written anything in it yet. I was saving it. But I often flipped through the empty pages, thinking about what I'd write.

Now I lifted the red cover with the dried flowers pressed inside.

The first page was missing.

I held the book closer to my face. Tiny rips were all that was left of the page where the inscription had been written. The page had been carefully torn out.

Your mom-to-be.

Mom-to-be. Mom-to-be.

It was if she had never been here.

I didn't cry. I wasn't ever going to cry again.

Part II

Chapter 25

It took me a real, real long time to even open the red journal Cleo had given me. At first, after she left, I was so upset I couldn't touch the book — not even to throw it out. Then I got this dumb note from her about three weeks after she left saying her leaving had nothing to do with me and she only tore out the inscription in a moment of panic and confusion, that I'd understand when I got older, or maybe I'd be lucky and never have to.

I never wrote back.

After a while the red journal seemed like just another blank book. But I would never write in it. And I'd never pull out the rest of that torn page. I'd keep it there, all jagged and ripped. Then by four and a half months later, I barely even thought about any of it, anymore. Honest.

I'd grown up a lot since then. It was too bad Kelly Noonan hadn't, though. She still wore only purple, with only one day off, when she wore all green for St. Patrick's Day. The next day she was right back to purple.

And Taylor and I were now totally best friends. YBFs.

We had a list of lines that we had to recite whenever one of us started the sequence. So far we had, in order:

I looove the chocolate glaze.

Got milk?

Hurry, get a paper towel.

And then one day Taylor and I were standing in the bus line to go to my house after school. There were three late bus routes for kids who stayed after, but some days, like that day, there were only a few of us waiting.

"You guys have to dress alike, too?" Peter said. He was in the line next to ours waiting for his bus to show up.

Taylor and I both looked at each other at the same time to see what Peter was talking about. We hadn't even planned it, and we hadn't noticed it all day. Taylor was wearing white overalls, a blue T-shirt, and a white sweat jacket. I had on blue jeans and a white T-shirt with a blue windbreaker. The exact reverse and the exact same thing.

"YBFs!" Taylor stood back to admire our clothing and how good we looked together. How two good friends naturally chose the same colors on the same day. YBFs.

"I didn't say you were elves," Peter said, shaking his head and holding up his hand in a gesture of disbelief.

We both looked at him, Taylor and I. It took a minute and then we broke out laughing at what Peter thought he had heard. Y:why. B:be. Fs:Elves?

"Why be elves?" Taylor asked me, as if this question had seriously just occurred to her.

"Why not?" I answered.

And then that was one of our lines. Just simply, *Why be elves?*

Peter was still shaking his head at us out his bus window while Taylor and I ran through our lines (now four of them) and laughed. Another bus arrived and the rest of the students went home. It was only Taylor and me left waiting.

"Hey, Gabby?" Taylor said quietly.

"Yeah?"

"Is there anything I should know for when I get my period? That is, if I *ever* get my period," Taylor said.

There wasn't much to know, I told Taylor. Just that it doesn't come the same time every month even though they said that in the movie. And it doesn't hurt or anything. And it's no big deal, really, after the first time, after the first hour or so.

Mr. Worthington finally appeared in his big, yellow bus, rounding the turn into the school.

"Gabby?"

"Yeah?"

"Well, when I do get it, I don't want to tell anyone till I tell you." Taylor finished quickly before the bus arrived.

"Really?"

"You're my YBF," Taylor said.

"And you're mine," I said.

Chapter 26

Ian stood by the door, ready to leave for school, and commented on the river. Even though I was the only other person in the kitchen, I wasn't sure that he was talking to me.

"By tomorrow the bus will have to go around the long way," he said.

I looked out the window. It was only six-thirty in the morning, and already the sun was fully risen. The Wall-kill was threatening to spill over its banks due to melting snow from the surrounding mountains and unusually wet weather. When that happens, water rushes over the low flats of the cornfields and the low roads. The police come around with orange barricades to divert traffic all the way around, almost to Rosendale. Water rushes up all around our property, because our house is built on a slight hill. Only the house and our driveway stay dry. The grass of our lawn gets laid flat and wet under a thin layer of murky water. Already the trees just beside the river were covered midway up their trunks.

"Maybe even by this afternoon," Ian said.

I couldn't tell if he was glad or unhappy or worried by this. Like most things, he simply reported it. Just as Ian had never mentioned Cleo again, not even to say her name. But, like I said, after four and a half months you can forget anything.

"I bet by this afternoon they'll block off our road," Ian said as he walked out the door to catch the bus to the high school.

I wasn't taking the bus that morning. My dad was taking me to his office with him so I could get pool passes for the college pool. I had invited my best friend, also known as Taylor Such, YBF, to come swimming with me Saturday when my dad had all-day classes. I had told my dad all week that if I didn't get the passes by Friday, the administration offices would be closed.

He might have been slow and disorganized, but my dad usually came through.

We got to the college early. I waited in the studio-art office while my dad did something he said he was supposed to have done the week before, of course. Then we could go to the administration building and get the pool passes, he promised.

The magazines in the office were really bad, *Art Times* and *Arts in Review*. Nothing I wanted to read. I kept looking up at the clock on the wall, because if my dad didn't get back soon I was going to be late for school.

I stared at everything in the room to pass the time and finally focused on the secretary, who sat typing at her computer.

"Hi, Robin!" Someone's voice flew in through the open door to the office. By the time the secretary looked up to wave, the person was gone. But she had looked up just in time to catch me staring at her.

"Your father should be back any minute, honey," Robin told me with a fake smile.

She resumed typing at her computer. She had two bracelets on each arm and three rings on each hand. As her fingers hit the keys, the bracelets clicked and the rings danced up and down. That's when I noticed her fingernails. They were painted white. Short and perfectly square.

I picked up the copy of *Art Times* and held it to my face. Then I slowly brought my hands around, kept them low so as to be inconspicuous, and turned them over to inspect my own nails. I bite my fingernails, not so much out of nervousness, but as sort of a Gabby Weiss manicure. It keeps them short, but jagged and certainly not white. Not pretty, not a girl's hands, not like Robin's.

"How do you get your nails so pretty?" I asked.

Robin stopped typing, looked up, and glanced around the room to see who I was talking to.

Duh.

"Oh, thank you," she said finally.

Robin apparently didn't realize that what I really wanted was an answer. She was still smiling that dumb smile. I was still waiting.

"Gelatin," she said, finally catching on. "I buy these packets of gelatin in the grocery store and I mix it in with a glass of water and I drink it."

This was list-journal information.

"Oh," I said. "Thanks."

"Your dad should be out any minute now," Robin said again.

I made her nervous.

As soon as my dad returned, we went to get the passes. I made it to school on time, and as soon as I saw her in the hall I snuck a look at Taylor's nails. They were neatly filed and shiny, pinkish-clear.

I knew that if Mrs. Tyler thought it was important for Taylor, she would be the first to run out, buy the gelatin, and mix it up every morning for her daughter's breakfast. Maybe she already did.

"What are you looking at?" Taylor asked me.

"Nothing."

I had told Taylor a lot lately, but not everything.

I hadn't told her about my list. I hadn't told her about my mother. I hadn't told her it was my fault that my mother had died.

"No, really, what are you looking at?" Taylor nudged me with her elbow.

"You have nice nails," I told Taylor, "that's all," and we headed to our homeroom.

When I got home that afternoon, my dad was outside checking the groundwater situation. The grassy fields that led directly to the river were saturated. My dad stood in the path he himself had cut and shifted his weight from foot to foot. He looked like he was on a seesaw you couldn't see. He was grumbling again.

The septic. Damn. The well. Damn it.

Whatever that river was carrying, it couldn't hold much longer. The ground was full, the water was as high as it could get, and eventually everything would spill out, like stories that have to be told.

Chapter 27

It was Saturday. Mrs. Tyler had agreed (way in advance) to pick me up from my house after lunch and then drop Taylor and me off at the college. My dad was going to pick us up after we went swimming, after he was done with his classes, and take Taylor home. My dad even had to talk to Mrs. Tyler on the phone about all these plans. Which he did. And Mrs. Tyler was right on time.

"Are you sure this is the right place?" Mrs. Tyler asked twice, even though the words SUNY NEW PALTZ MEMOR-IAL GYMNASIUM were nailed to the wall of this huge, brick building.

"You've been here before?" she asked. "You've done this before?"

"Millions of times," I said. But to be perfectly honest, I hadn't ever gone to the college gym without a grown-up before.

"We're fine, Mom," Taylor said firmly. We both got out of the car.

Taylor had to wave to her mother again from inside

the big window of the gym, and finally Mrs. Tyler drove away.

I hadn't even been swimming here in probably two years, not since my dad used to take me and Ian on hot summer days, before they built the new town pool out by the high school. I was hoping, I was praying, I would remember where the women's lockers were and wouldn't look like I didn't know what I was doing.

When my dad took us, he used to take me into the men's room and shuttle me right out through the showers to the pool. We always came already dressed in our bathing suits. But the last time I came with my dad and Ian, I insisted on walking through the women's room to get to the pool. (Or rather, I refused to walk, or even run, through the men's locker room.) The thought of naked men horrified me, and Ian told me those college students always walked around naked like nobody's business. It is something that happens to you when you get to college, he said. You lose your fear of being nude.

I thought of that as Taylor and I headed for the women's locker room. I somehow remembered the right direction: down the steps, to the right past the squash courts. The vending machines were new. Taylor must have been a little nervous, too, or she picked it up from me. She walked a little slower as we got near the door.

WOMEN'S LOCKER ROOM.

Just as I reached for the handle, the door swung open and a college woman came out. We nearly banged into her.

She seemed startled, but she didn't say anything. Her hair was combed but totally wet. She smelled of soap and chlorine as she passed by. She looked so grown-up, and I imagined she had been naked just a few minutes before. If I thought about this too long, I was going to chicken out.

"Go ahead," I said, holding the door for Taylor.

Inside, the smell of chlorine was even greater. The warm steam from the showers and cold air from the hall met right at the position by the door where Taylor and I stood. Women of all sizes were walking around — women in all stages of getting dressed and undressed. Breasts bobbed and bare bottoms walked by.

I started straight down a long row of lockers and benches and found an empty corner close to the pool entrance. We scooted far down the bench against the wall.

I knew if I looked at Taylor I was going to laugh nervously and loud and the whole locker room would echo. All around us metal lockers banged closed and reverberated. Showers ran, toilets flushed, wet footsteps padded. None of the women were talking much, but it was hollow and loud with locker-room noise.

Both Taylor and I began undressing in that girl way, which I learned last year in fifth grade when we had to change for gym. At first I had to watch the other girls getting into their gym clothes; arms pulled out of shirts but still completely covering their bodies, shirts covering their legs while they pulled off their pants. I wrote it down on my list. Now I, too, am able to completely change my clothes without being undressed for a single moment.

"Where do we put our clothes?" Taylor asked me. She was in her bathing suit with her oversized towel tightly wrapped around her waist. It hung almost to her feet. I was busy covering up my own body, wearing a big sweatshirt with my swimsuit underneath.

"In any locker that's empty," I said.

Most of the lockers had padlocks dangling, but we each found an unused one, stuffed all our things quickly inside, and slammed it shut again.

"Ready?" I asked.

I had my bathing suit from last year. I hadn't thought much about it when I grabbed it from my drawer that morning, but now it felt tight.

"Leave your sweatshirt here," Taylor said. "Just use your towel like me. I've got to use the bathroom first. Where is it?"

I pointed. At least the stalls had doors on them that closed.

"Wait for me," Taylor ordered as she shut the swinging door and I heard the lock slide into place.

I reopened my locker, slipped my sweatshirt off, and threw it in. I wrapped the towel around my waist as Taylor suggested and I stepped out from the bench aisle to wait for Taylor by the bathroom. I heard her struggling to pull down her suit.

There were mirrors at the end of each row. I caught a

glimpse of myself as I waited. Since no one was around, I dropped my towel a little. I dared to take a tiny look at myself. Maybe I could see if my hips were starting to get big. I faced backward and tried to twist my head all the way around and see myself from behind. But that hurt my neck too much. I straightened myself out and looked again.

Something looked wrong. My bathing suit was tight, but that didn't account for the soft skin visible below both shoulder straps. Flesh that had started as the small beginnings of breasts now reached up toward my underarms. And the material of my bathing suit no longer covered it.

"What's wrong?" Taylor had come out and stood beside me.

I wanted to hide, but there was no place to go. I looked at Taylor's body beside me in the mirror. Her chest was still flat, her torso square; no flesh softened her angular ribs and slipped out for the world to see.

"What?" Taylor said again.

I didn't want to call attention to something she hadn't noticed yet. My first thought was to put my shirt back on. Make an excuse and never go swimming again as long as I live. As I stared at myself, I began to look more and more wrong.

For the second time since I had known Taylor, she did something remarkable. She put her arm around me and asked again. Softly.

"Gabby, tell me," she said. "What's wrong?"

So I told her. And standing in that locker room looking into the mirror, neither one of us could figure it out.

"Well," Taylor began, "let's look around."

"No way!"

"Just casually," Taylor instructed, "like we're just taking a little walk to the sink to wash our hands." She lowered her voice.

So we walked casually over to the long line of sinks. I
turned on the water. Two women walked behind me.
One in sweats and the other in a bathing suit. The one in
the bathing suit was tall and very muscular, but just
around her arms and chest she was round and soft.

Another woman walked by wearing nothing on top at
all. I looked away as fast as I could and then looked back.
She was very round and jiggled and had white, round
flesh from her breasts to her underarms. It was not
grotesque. It was not a deformity. They were women.

We watched a few more women, fat and thin, flat and
large breasted, big and small, and it seemed that for
some, this skin was an extension of their breasts. When
we were at least partially satisfied that I was at least nearly
normal, we decided to head for the pool.

Neither of us said a word. We immediately jumped
into the shallow end, without even testing the tempera-
ture of the water. Without the usual squeals and screams
that come from dunking one toe in at a time.

"God, my hands are shaking," Taylor said, emerging
from a dolphin dive just next to me.

"Why? If it was you, you could have just gone home

and asked your mother." I wiped the water from my eyes.

"My mother!" Taylor practically shouted. "My mother! My mother says she's 'having a visit from her friend' when she has her period. When my Aunt Judy was pregnant, my mother couldn't even say it. She told me Aunt Judy was 'in the family way'!"

"A visit from her friend?" I started laughing.

"My mother has to run the water in the sink while she's peeing so nobody can hear! My mother won't let me see her underpants in the laundry."

I was laughing; pool water was dripping from my hair.

"So you see, YBF, it's not what you think. I really couldn't just go home and ask my mother," Taylor said. She tipped her head all the way back and let the water neatly comb the hair off her face. "Anyway, my mother does all the asking in my family."

"Well, at least you have a mother." But even as I said it, nothing seemed as clear as it once had.

I bent my knees and I let the water swallow me up. My body felt weightless, as close to flying as I could ever be. When I came up for air, Taylor was looking right at me.

"Gabby, tell me what really happened to your mother," she said quietly, swimming toward me.

Chapter 28

So I finally told Taylor the story about my mother, because that's all it was. A story.

I told Taylor that my brother and I got up one morning and couldn't wake our mother up. We were really little then, so neither of us can really remember her. We went down in the elevator to the doorman, but it is only a vague memory, I told her.

I told Taylor that my mother's accident was an overdose of sleeping pills. My mother had wanted to sleep a little more in the morning, and since I was so noisy and loud she needed to take more, but she took too many more by mistake. So it was partially my fault.

That's the story. She died.

"So where was your father?" Taylor asked right away.

"What?"

"Where was your father? Didn't he know something was wrong? Why did he let you and Ian go by yourselves in the elevator?"

I didn't have an answer for this. My father wasn't part of the story. It was just as I told it. My brother and I tried to wake our mother up and we couldn't. We rode in an elevator. That's the story.

"Didn't you ever ask him?" Taylor went on.

"Who?" I asked. I was feeling a chill from my wet hair as we sat on the curb outside the gym and waited for my dad to pick us up.

"Ask your dad. Didn't you ever ask him what happened? Where was he?"

"Why don't you ask your own self questions?" I snapped at Taylor.

"What do you mean?"

"Like where was Richard all that time your parents were married and buying real estate. Didn't you say you've known Richard from before your parents got divorced? So your mother knew Richard while she was married to your dad, didn't she?"

Taylor looked at me, with confusion in her face. And hurt. At least she wasn't asking any more questions.

That afternoon, as Ian predicted, the Wallkill River flooded its banks. The barricades went up. We had to drive home the long way around.

I stopped writing in my list journal that night, forever. The things I needed to know to be a woman were more complex than I originally had thought. It was more than how to train your bangs or how to cross your legs. It was more than I knew, or even Taylor knew.

I stuck my list journal under my coloring books (the

fancy kind of coloring books, of movie stars and famous women, not the baby cartoon kind) and left it there. My last entry was the one about fingernails and powdered gelatin.

My dad was getting more and more agitated by the flooding river. He got up in the middle of the night with a flashlight and checked everything. Each and every thing. He came into my room to check on me, I suppose. I wouldn't have even known he had been in my room except that in the morning I saw the clothes I had left on the floor hanging over the back of my chair.

It reminded me that Cleo must have come into my room when I was sleeping to tear that page out of my red book. And then to top it off, I had a really bad dream that night.

I dreamt that I was running across the flooded ground flapping my arms wildly. Just when I thought I was about to take off into the air, I suddenly got stuck in the thick mud and I couldn't move at all. I couldn't run and I couldn't fly.

I made sure to write down what I could remember in my dream journal in the morning, but I still had an uneasy feeling. I knew it had something to do with all that talking I did with Taylor after swimming. Talking can stir things up in your mind like that. Another mystery of the mind.

But it was no mystery that I had been really mean to Taylor.

*A*s soon as I got to school, I had to run and find Taylor and apologize. She was by the main office.

"I'm sorry," I said right off the bat.

I'm not used to apologizing; admitting I was wrong when I really don't want to admit that. And besides, you never know what kind of reaction you're going to get. But this time I really meant it more than I cared how Taylor would feel about me or how I felt about myself.

"I shouldn't have said that stuff about your mom and your stepfather," I said.

"I'm sorry, too, for asking about your mother," Taylor said. "You obviously don't want to talk about it and I pushed you."

True.

"You were right, though," Taylor went on.

"About what?"

We started down the hall for our first class.

"My mom *was* seeing Richard before she and my dad got divorced. I knew it then. I knew the whole time."

I looked around at everyone passing us in the halls, all the other kids heading to their classes. All with their own embarrassing stories, probably. Still, out of some kind of instinct, I felt ashamed for her. I moved closer to Taylor so we could talk more softly as we walked.

"I never told my dad." Taylor watched her feet as she talked and walked. "Maybe if I had . . ."

"You can't think even for one minute that it's your fault your parents got divorced," I said to Taylor.

Taylor stopped at the door to our homeroom. She didn't need to say anything this time. I knew she didn't really think she was to blame, but maybe if she had said something to her dad, maybe it would have been different.

It was the same with me. I sort of knew it wasn't really my fault that my mother had taken an overdose of sleeping pills, but then again I sort of knew it was.

Chapter 29

My dad was in his studio when I got home from school. I opened the back door of the garage to the familiar smells of oil paint and turpentine. I would ask him here. About my mother. I would ask him why he didn't do anything that morning my mother died. Why we went alone in the elevator.

It is important to confront my dad in his own territory. I remembered once Ian wanting something or another for his guitar or his amp and trying to ask Dad for it while we were eating at a restaurant.

I could have told Ian right then and there it wasn't going to work. Outside of his natural surroundings my dad can't think straight, so he gets cranky. "No" is about all he can say when he can't think straight.

I stepped inside the studio. My dad wasn't painting. His paint table was wiped clean. White glass, not a drop of color. The easel stood empty, not even a sketch pad for a charcoal study. All the tubes of oils were carefully put away, brushes sorted by function and drying; scrapers, pencils, and charcoals in an old coffee can. There was only a lingering smell from when he had been painting regularly. He still spent a lot of time out there, but he wasn't whistling so good these days.

And it was dark. Only the light over his desk was on. My dad was bent over and writing. He stopped when I came in. "Hi, sweetie," he said. "How was school?"

"Fine."

When I didn't directly cross and go through the kitchen door, my dad closed his notebook. He put down his pencil. I sat down on the hooked rug that covered most of the cold, concrete floor.

For a long while I didn't say anything. I listened to the hum of the house, the electric buzzing noises that are always running in the background. It all seemed the same as it had always been, just like Ian said. The three of us. Why would I want to go and ruin that?

"Dad?" I began.

"Hmm?" my dad, too, was staring quietly into space, perhaps listening to the same comforting sounds of a house standing still.

And then Taylor's voice:

Where was your father?

Didn't he know something was wrong?

I looked at my dad sitting in the same chair where he always sat. He cleared his throat. Everything the same as I always remembered it. Safe. Why would I want to go and ruin something like that?

"Nothing," I said.

I uncrossed my legs and stood up. I opened the door to where natural light filled the kitchen and walked inside the house. Ian was home, sprawled on the couch. His guitar was right beside him but he wasn't playing. The TV was on, an empty package of Fig Newtons was on the coffee table.

"You pig," I said. I was joking. I don't even like Fig Newtons.

"There were only a few left," Ian defended himself. He kept his focus on the TV.

"Anyway, *you're* the pig," he said. "There was a whole box two days ago, and I've only had seven. Four yesterday and three today."

Who counts their cookies? I thought. Ian does. He counts everything. He measures all time. He demands all fairness. He hoards up TV minutes from days before and he's mean.

"What's your problem, anyway?" I shouted. "Why do you pick on me so much? What did I ever do to you?"

I suppose Ian could have come up with several incidents at that moment. He could have mentioned the time I warped his favorite CD by leaving it next to the heater, after listening to it without his permission. He could have recalled the time I told everyone at his eleven-year-old birthday party that Ian threw up in the car once when he was little, even though I hadn't even been there.

But he could be so mean, so mean to me.

I wanted to hit my brother over the head with the Fig

Newton box. I wanted to scream out loud forever or till I felt like stopping. I wanted to know everything he was holding inside and keeping from me.

"What's wrong with you?" Ian said. He finally had to look at me.

"You!" I said. "You're what's wrong with me! You're my big brother. You're supposed to take care of me. Look out for me." The sound of my own voice and my own words and my own anger scared me, but I continued. "You never do. You never did!"

Ian withdrew deeper into the cushions of the couch. He looked smaller, and all of a sudden I felt sad. I knew I was asking for something from someone who was as alone as I was. I felt like I had thrown an acorn right at the back of Ian's head and for the first time it hit him.

Still, I couldn't ask Dad. I had tried that.

"Why haven't you ever looked out for me?" I said. "Not since that day. Not since that day you took me in the elevator with you. Why did you even take me with you in the first place?"

It was hard to see Ian look so uncomfortable. For as much as I had fantasized about cutting my brother down to size, it was a size that frightened me.

"How could Dad have let you take me like that? And where were we going?" I asked. I had to know.

The TV was still on. Talking and canned laughter coming out from the set; cars screeching their tires; and then a commercial for hair gel.

"Dad wasn't there," Ian told me as he turned back to the TV screen. "We were the only ones in the apartment. I was going out to look for him, I guess. I don't know. We were alone."

There are stories you always hear, and stories you know you are making up; not quite lies, really. There are things you've always thought were true, maybe just because you've never thought about them in any other way. Things that don't make sense but you've never questioned them, and when you finally do, you can't understand how you could have accepted them for so long.

We were alone?

We wound up in Ian's room with the door shut. I don't think I had seen the inside of his room since I was five. At first I just kept looking at all his stuff. The cool CD rack that bent around like a wave, the posters, on every inch of every wall, of every musician Ian thought ever counted for anything. He had an incense burner, an ash tray (I didn't ask him what for), a major compact disc–and–dual tape player. He had ceramic bowls filled with different things, guitar picks in one, pennies in another, Snapple bottle tops in another.

"After we tried and we couldn't wake her up, we got in the elevator and went down to the lobby. We told the doorman our mother wouldn't wake up, but he didn't believe us. Didn't believe me," my brother told me.

"We were still in our pajamas, but we walked out into the street. Then we just went back in and waited. I don't remember what happened after that."

With his words, Ian painted a lonely picture of two little children in their sleeping clothes wandering around the halls of an apartment building in New York City.

"I didn't even think to call nine-one-one. The doorman told us to go back upstairs and let our mother sleep. Well, he was a grown-up, right?"

Is he asking me? I turned to look at Ian.

I wanted to reach over and touch Ian, the way Taylor could do for me, but I couldn't move. The door was shut, and I suddenly felt trapped. At the same time, I never wanted to leave this room, this moment. I wanted to go on talking, telling stories, sharing stories.

Chapter 30

Things were changing. It was spring. It was so bright in the mornings that I was usually up and ready for school as early as Ian was. He sometimes let me hold the controller while he watched TV before his bus came.

Even the table arrangements in the middle school cafeteria were breaking up. Things were changing. Amber Whitman no longer sat at the head of The Ones' table. Kelly, no longer in purple (I heard that her mother finally put her foot down), and Melanie sat together, but by themselves. They were best friends. And lately Amber was sitting with us. Us being of course me and Taylor and sometimes Peter. The boys' table was breaking up and sometimes one or two of them ventured over to sit with some of the girls. Sophie had a real boyfriend and they sat together.

Rhonda Littleman usually sat alone. Or with Alex, and they still thought they were better than everyone else. Which some things considered, they were.

It was spring.

But today the sky was dark. Rain threatened. I got my

hot lunch and scanned the cafeteria for a place to sit. Taylor had not come down yet. She had a special project she was working on in Spanish. I saw Lynette sitting all by herself, and I sat down right next to her.

"Hi, Lynette," I said.

She looked up. If she was surprised that I was sitting here she didn't show it.

"Hello," Lynette answered. I saw she had bought hot lunch, too.

"You know, Lynette. There's something I've really wanted to ask you." I started. We both had gotten the Chunky Turkey gravy with mashed potatoes.

"What, Gabby? What did you want to ask me?" I tried to ignore her pulling the pieces of turkey out and laying them on her tray in a line.

"How did you know that day, that day when Taylor first came. . . . How did you know she was going to cry?" I began.

"Well, I didn't know she was going to cry *again*." Lynette seemed to remember just what I was referring to.

"What do you mean 'again'?"

"I was in the office when her mother brought her in. She was crying," Lynette told me.

"But you said, 'She's coming and she'll cry,'" I said firmly. "I heard you. You said that."

Lynette shook her head. "I cry, too. Sometimes right in front of strangers."

"No, Lynette. Remember? You said, 'She's coming and

she'll cry.' Like she was going to cry, like you knew it before it happened," I said.

Lynette shrugged. "I don't remember."

Taylor had come in and she walked over with her bag lunch. She sat down beside Lynette. She didn't say anything. She just listened.

"Well, how did you know about the butter and milk and heavy cream and everything?" I asked Lynette.

"I watch the cooking channel with my grandmother." Lynette's face brightened. She looked at Taylor and then back to me. "Do you ever watch that channel?"

"I've seen it once," Taylor said.

Could I have been so wrong? Thinking she had visions or something? How stupid was I?

Suddenly, Lynette started waving her arms back and forth. I turned to see what she was looking at. Her friend, Lea Fry-O'Malley, was standing with her lunch tray and was obviously looking around for Lynette.

"Here, here," Lynette called out.

Before I knew it, I was sitting with Taylor and Lynette and Lea and Peter, who had wandered over. And then Amber.

The fluorescent lights hummed steadily. Talk and laughter rose and fell from the tables around us. Then a loud clap of thunder shook the walls and at that exact moment a burst of white light flashed outside the windows. A storm was directly on top of us. Rain began to bullet the roof of the school, and then all the lights went out.

A boom of thunder was followed by silence, and then laughter broke into the nervous quiet as everyone realized it had only been lightning that hit the building and knocked out the electricity.

"Awesome," Peter said.

"That must have just missed us," Amber said.

The rain was coming down hard and the sky was now almost black. Without the lights in the cafeteria it was darker inside than out.

"Or it just hit us," I said.

"Wow," Taylor said and lifted her eyebrows. "Will they send us home?"

I looked across the table to where Lynette sat quietly. I couldn't completely make out Lynette's face in the shadows, but I knew something was not right. Her eyes looked wild, scared. Then I saw Lynette slowly bend over like a little kid with a stomachache and shriek loudly once. Just like at the assembly back in October.

Amber, who was sitting on the other side of Lynette, nearly jumped out of her seat. Peter and I exchanged looks, but neither one of us knew what to do. Lynette began shrieking steadily. Slowly the rest of the people in the darkened cafeteria stopped talking till all there was to hear were Lynette's cries.

Taylor tried to put her arm around Lynette. She talked softly, as you would to a frightened animal or a small child. But Lynette recoiled from Taylor's touch. She continued to cry and occasionally broke out with a loud, frightening scream.

Miss Crosby showed up first. The gym teacher and the two cafeteria ladies arrived seconds later.

"We got her," Miss Crosby said to Taylor. "Thank you."

Miss Crosby turned out to be very strong. She nearly lifted Lynette up from her fetal position in her chair. Then the gym teacher helped. They carried Lynette right out of the cafeteria, still crying. Miss Crosby was saying things to Lynette but wasn't touching her, as if she knew not to from past experience.

Just as they left, the lights went back on. But the room stayed quiet for another few minutes. Slowly the cafeteria came back to life with the ordinary sounds of eating and smashing milk cartons, putting away trays and garbage.

"Is that what happens when you get hit by a truck when you're a baby?" Peter asked, the first at our table to speak.

I narrowed my eyes at him. "That's such a stupid thing to say."

Peter looked sorry. Boys are mostly so stupid, but at least Peter knew it.

"Anyway, she wasn't hit by a truck," I told everyone. "She was left in an incubator when she was born and the doctor forgot to turn on the oxygen for a few seconds." My information was authentic and I could hardly stop myself from feeling proud to be the only one who knew it.

Amber, Taylor, and Peter all looked duly interested.

"But that's not true," Lea said. Until then no one had really noticed she was still there with us.

"She told me that herself," I told Lea firmly.

"Lynette tells stories," Lea said. "The first time I went to her grandmother's house, Lynette told me she was adopted as a baby from Bosnia."

I don't think I had talked to Lea Fry-O'Malley since second grade when she put my sneakers on by mistake after we did barefoot prints in art class. I know Amber Whitman *never* had. Now we were all here at the same table listening to Lea Fry-O'Malley. Things had certainly changed.

"So?" Peter prompted. He slid down to be closer to her and we followed.

"So her mother did it to her. She used to lock Lynette in the closet," Lea told us matter-of-factly. "That's why she has to live with her grandmother. Her grandmother doesn't want her, either, but the state took Lynette away from her mother."

"Is that why she gets so scared in the dark?" I said, putting the two incidents together, the darkness at the assembly and the power outage here in the cafeteria, knowing this was the truth.

"Yeah," Lea said. "She used to get locked in a closet for a long time. Sometimes for days."

No one said anything more. We finished eating.

Pretty soon the lights came back. The bell rang and lunch period was over. We all got up and headed to where we were supposed to be. Gratefully.

Then I saw Lynette in the nurse's office on my way to

last-period math class. She was sitting on the little cot by the wall.

"Lynette, are you all right?" I peeked in.

"Oh, Gabby. Yeah, why? I just have a little headache so I came to the nurse. I get headaches sometimes."

Lynette didn't even remember screaming. She didn't want to. That's when I knew. I had believed, as Lynette believed, in the stories because they were easy. Because they were stories.

The storm had ended in a drizzle of rain and then disappeared altogether.

"I get headaches because I was in an incubator when I was born," Lynette said, "and the doctor forgot to turn the oxygen on."

"Oh, that's really sad, Lynette," I said. And I meant it.

Chapter 31

By dismissal the sun was radiating off every wet, glistening object it could find. If it weren't for the puddles you would have never known there had just been a thunderstorm.

Taylor was coming over after school. Normally, we went to one of our houses after school every day. On weekends we had sleepovers. But this Friday, Taylor had to leave right before dinner because she was going to her dad's for the weekend and her mom wanted her home early.

We rode the bus to my house, along the road to the Rosendale Bridge, the long way since the road was still blocked, although parts of the river were beginning to recede. All along the road trees marked the river's highest point with a thick coating of mud circling their trunks. My house sat as if it were abandoned in the center of a bog, with one long dirt road trailing straight into it.

"Cool," Taylor said, looking around as we stepped down off the bus.

I waved to Mr. Worthington and we started walking down my driveway. Our backyard had disappeared into a horizon of shallow water.

"It's eerie. It's like another world," Taylor said.

We crossed the wet fields to cut off some of my driveway and headed to the front of the house. We listened to our feet squish loudly, our socks soaking up the warm water. The air was still and muggy and tiny mayflies buzzed around our sweaty skin.

"Everything is so gross," I commented, watching my sneakers turn dark with wetness.

"Except for right there!" Taylor pointed. "Look!"

She hurried ahead to the deeper grass, closer to the river itself, grass that had just recently been exposed to the air again. Brown silt clung to each weed and stick and in every crevice. All but one small tip of one small object that glittered back up to the shining sun. Taylor bent down and picked it up.

It was my butterfly barrette. One of them.

"Oooh. Look, it's beautiful," Taylor said. She tried to clean it with her hands. The mud just smeared.

"Hey, that's my barrette," I told her.

I never had to tell Taylor about Cleo. Cleo was gone just as Taylor and I were becoming best friends. Taylor never knew enough about Cleo to ask questions. Cleo. Even thinking her name seemed strange. I was trying to imagine how my barrette could have gotten so far up here. And how did it get unearthed? The river washed it all the way up here?

"I lost them a long time ago. There were two," I said. "So funny, here's one of them."

"I never saw you wear anything like this." Taylor was rubbing the barrette against her shirt.

"Well, I never actually wore them."

The butterfly was nearly sparkling again. I remembered when Cleo insisted on buying them for me, just because she wanted to. I felt a stinging in my eyes and my throat for a second, before I could push it away.

"So how did you lose them if you never wore them?" Taylor asked.

"All right," I said. We neared the front door of my house. "I wore them once, for a short time, and then I lost them."

"Did you ever bother looking for them? This one's beautiful."

I opened the back door to my house and spoke to the air and the bicycles hanging in the garage. "I didn't even remember that I had them. Why would I look for something I forgot all about!?"

We went inside.

My dad wasn't in the studio and Ian wasn't to be seen when we walked into the kitchen. Taylor left the barrette on the counter, as a sign, I hoped, that she would stop asking about it.

"Want something to eat?" I asked Taylor. I went to find something to offer her.

Taylor and I could hear the faint sound of the guitar coming from Ian's closed bedroom door.

"Is that Ian?" Taylor asked.

I pretended not to notice, but I could tell that Taylor was a little too interested in my brother. But since Ian had been nicer to me lately, I was okay with it. To a point.

Then I heard the music of an electric bass, too. *Ian must have someone over practicing with him*, I thought. *Paul?*

My stomach tightened, warning me that stupid things were potentially going to come out of my mouth. I closed the pantry doors.

"Is that Ian playing?" Taylor asked again. She headed toward the music.

"Well, it's not me," I said. I followed her into the living room, toward the muffled sounds, toward Ian's room.

The music was actually drifting out Ian's window and in again through the big, open screen doors in the living room. Then the music abruptly stopped as the door of Ian's bedroom banged open and Paul stepped out. He turned directly to where Taylor and I stood gawking. He stopped.

"We just got home," I said to Paul, breaking my own record for saying the stupidest thing imaginable.

Paul looked at us. "Oh, that's nice," he said.

Then, just when I thought I couldn't say anything stupider, Taylor did.

"We rode the school bus," Taylor said.

"Oh," Paul said, wrinkling his brow. He was very tall.

The door behind Paul slowly creaked open further, and there was my brother, sitting on the bed, one foot on the floor, his guitar in his hands, sheet music resting on his one folded knee.

"Hi, Gab. Hi, Taylor." The pencil he was holding in his mouth dropped out. "Dad just called and said he'll be home any minute."

"Uh, can I get by?" Paul asked.

Oh, my God. Paul had been trying to get by me all along, not standing around so he could talk to us.

"Oh, sure," I said and quickly stepped aside, and Paul moved through the space that I had just been standing in.

And that was it.

Ian got up to follow. He told me that he and Paul had to go into town. He said to tell Dad he'd be back before supper. They left in Paul's van, which I would have seen in the driveway if we hadn't cut across the tall grass, gotten our sneakers soaked, and found the barrette.

"He's cute," Taylor said. We were sitting and watching TV and coloring in my new *Movies Stars of the 30s and 40s* coloring book.

"Yeah," I said. I thought Paul was cute, but I would never have said it first.

"No, I mean your brother." By this point in our friendship Taylor knew more what I was saying than I did.

"I think Ian's cute," Taylor said as she busied herself

with Jean Harlow, Blond Bombshell, filling in her hair canary yellow.

"Is he?" I asked. I was working on Claudette Colbert. Short brown hair. Star of *It Happened One Night*, I read.

We had had cookies and potato chips already. And iced tea. My dad had come home and he was out back working in his garden. He'd probably stay outside till he decided to defrost some frozen dinners or order a pizza.

"Well, I think so," Taylor said, still talking about my brother.

We colored in silence for a while. Then I asked Taylor if she wanted me to get us a Fruit Roll-Up.

"No, thanks. But you're lucky," Taylor said. She put down her colored pencil. "My mother practically measures everything that goes into my mouth."

"Lucky?" I stopped coloring. Should I be worrying about what I eat, too? I thought I remembered that was on my list somewhere: Watch your weight. Don't eat too many sweets.

"Oh . . . I didn't mean you're lucky you don't have a mother," Taylor quickly added. "I mean, lucky that you don't have someone breathing down your back all the time. . . . But . . . I guess . . . I didn't mean that how it sounded."

"I wasn't even thinking *that*, Taylor," I told her. "Wanna switch?" I turned the page to Bette Davis on one side of the spread-open coloring book and Maureen O'Hara on the other.

"But I think it's really, really sad you lost your mother when you were so little," Taylor went on.

"I didn't *lose* my mother," I said. "She died."

Taylor started coloring Bette Davis. "But you *lost* her, too. My grandmother died a few years ago, but my dad and I talk about her all the time. . . . So it's like we still have her."

A one-dimensional Maureen O'Hara stood with her hands resting delicately on her legs. She was in a plain bathing suit with two outfits free-standing beside her. One outfit was a Tarzan dress. She looked out from the page at me with a gray smile. I'd never heard of Maureen O'Hara. And here she was in a book. I read the short caption below her picture. When she was born, where she lived, what movies she made.

I now knew more about Maureen O'Hara than I did about my own mother. I could close this book and remember her face and this little bit of information, and I could even go to the video store and rent a movie with her in it.

"Wouldn't it be funny if I could find my mother, sort of," I said out loud. "Sort of . . . like we found that barrette. . . ."

Like we found that barrette. The thought grabbed me hard, like a strong fist; I knew it was not going to let go.

But how can I look for something I don't even remember having?

And then it occurred to me — I don't remember my mother because I was so young, but also I don't remember *having* a mother.

And that's what I'd lost.

I had lost the chance to reminisce, to remember and tell stories. To remember someone just because you keep talking about them; learn about someone by hearing things like "Oh, your mother used to hold her knife just like that" or "Your mother hated the way her hair flipped up, too," or "Your mother used to love to sing in the car just like . . ."

I'd only lost a memory, only the story, and a story is something you could find. It's got to be all in there somewhere, a dream, like a mystery of the mind. You just need to know where to look. Or how.

What if I could? I wondered why I hadn't thought of it before. Had I spent so much time keeping lists and journals when all along I could have been looking?

Remembering?

"What if I could just go and look for her?" I think I said that out loud.

The feeling welled up inside me like a huge possibility. It gave me a tremble inside like when you're standing on top of a very high ladder, looking down, feeling like you're going to fall, knowing you are probably going to fall, but wondering all the same if maybe you could fly.

"Well, when I'm looking for something I've lost, I try all the places I usually put things," Taylor said. She stopped coloring.

"I run around the house like crazy tearing everything apart, pulling out drawers, throwing things on the ground," I said.

"I ask my mother where she put whatever I'm looking for, because she is always moving things and then I can't find anything." Taylor had closed the coloring book now.

"Well, after I've tried everything else, I go back to the place I know I last had it," I said.

Chapter 32

Taylor's mother had long since picked Taylor up, Stouffer's mac and cheese dinners had been microwaved and eaten, and everyone had gone to bed. But not to sleep. At least not me.

I lay in my bed and listened to my eyelashes fluttering against my pillow. I flipped around, stuck out my feet, and pulled them back under the covers. Left side, right side. Stomach. I tried to conjure up the image of a mother, my mother, walking out of a New York City apartment building. Pushing a stroller? Carrying her pocketbook over her shoulder? Apparently the mystery of my mind was a blank. I would have to go back. Literally.

I took my photo album off my shelf and fumbled through the pages. *Here. It's here.* I ran into my brother's dark room and told him my idea.

"You want to do what?" Ian asked me, rubbing his eyes.

"I want to go to four thirty-five East Seventy-ninth Street," I repeated. "It's right here. It's the address. It's where we lived when our mother died."

I was holding her driver's license, which, I remembered, had an address on it. Her address. Our address. I was waving it in my brother's face, a face that had been sleeping just a few seconds before.

"What do you want to do that for? That's ridiculous." Ian sat up and flipped on the light beside his bed, a black light. It didn't brighten the room much but all his posters came to life, reaching out from the walls in lime greens and pinks. It made the white T-shirt Ian slept in glow like it was plugged in.

"I just want to," I said. "I want to go back to the last place I know she existed; at least for me. Maybe you, too. And see if I can remember anything."

I sat down on the floor. I crossed my legs, like a kindergartner at circle time. "I mean, there's got to be something way deep in my brain. Rhonda Littleman did a report on that called 'The Mysteries of the Mind.' Everything you've ever seen or said or done is in your brain somewhere, even if you can't remember it."

"Rhonda Littleman?" Ian said sarcastically. "I guess this really is serious."

"Never mind," I said as I stood up. "I don't even know why I came in here. I just thought you'd be interested. I'm going tomorrow. On the train. Don't tell Dad. Anyway, he's got his first-Saturday-of-the-month class. I'll be back before he even gets home."

Ian grabbed the shirt of my pajamas as I started to leave. I could feel his fingers on my back where he held on. His touch was startling. So unfamiliar. Ian never touched me.

"How are you going to do this?" he demanded.

"I just am," I said.

"How are you even going to get to the train station? It's in Poughkeepsie," Ian said. "It's half an hour away. By car!"

"So?" I said, just like Oprah recommended. This time it worked. Ian had no response.

I walked back to my room. I crawled under my covers, which I had left warm but were now empty and chilly. At some point I must have fallen asleep, because the next thing I remember it was Saturday morning.

The sun was clearly shining. In the flooding water over our lawn the sky was reflected as glassy blue, even formations of white clouds could be seen by looking down at where the ground used to be. I was planning my trip. I had Plan A and Plan B. Plan A: Call the cab company and find out how much it would be to get to the train station from New Paltz. And B: If a cab was too much, go into town, forge my dad's signature, and cash one of my U.S. savings bonds. Then call the cab company. Then go to the train station. Then go to New York. Then find apartment. Come home.

"Will you be home today?" My dad's voice startled me from my reverie.

"What?"

I turned away from the window and saw my dad. He had a cup of coffee in one hand and his briefcase under the same arm.

"It's the first Saturday of the month. I'll be at the college all day," my dad said resignedly. "We've got to review portfolios."

"That sounds like fun."

"Well, the reviews are boring and listening to the other faculty talk about the reviews is even more boring, but other than that it's loads of fun," he said. He put down his coffee and looked at his watch.

"Then why are you going?" Ian was up unusually early for Ian. He walked into the kitchen and had his eyes on me.

"Why?" My dad began to answer. "To make a living, that's why, and besides, I have nothing better to do with my time since . . . since . . . you know." He cut himself off.

He wouldn't even say her name. So I shouted it inside my brain — *Since CLEO.*

And then I shouted ME inside. So quietly.

ME, Dad. ME. Look at me.

"I'll see you when I get home," my dad said, then kissed the top of my head.

"Bye, Dad," I said.

As soon as I heard my dad's car leave the driveway, I turned to Ian and said, "I'm still going. Don't try and stop me."

I had prepared myself for Ian to make fun of me. To dismiss my mission as so dramatic and ridiculous that only I could have thought of it. I know that if he had done that, he might have convinced me. I might have chickened out. Then how many things would never have happened the way they did?

"I already called Paul and asked him to drive us to the train," Ian said. He poured himself a cup of coffee from the machine Dad had just flipped off. I tried to think if I had seen Ian drink coffee before. "Hurry and we can catch the eight fifty-five."

"We?" I asked once and not again.

I needed Ian and I knew it. And he knew it.

Chapter 33

The train rocked us back and forth and clicked over the tracks like a metronome counting out measures.

I was afraid to look at Ian.

The round-trip tickets cost us each $24.24. The taxi to the apartment on 79th Street would probably be another five or ten, Ian figured. We could walk back to Grand Central, and with food and maybe a drink this whole thing was costing. Really costing.

As we moved farther and farther away from Pough-keepsie (Ian was right, I could *never* have walked to the train station, even with two days' supplies and a sleeping bag), I watched out the window streaked with grease, inside and out. We were passing through towns so quickly I could hardly focus on the lives taking place on the platforms, people waiting, strange faces seen and then gone. We were on the Croton/Harlem express straight to 125th Street and then Grand Central, New York City. Ian and I were facing backward; in front of us a businessman sat hidden by his newspaper. He, facing forward. I heard voices all around, some louder than others; male, female, all muffled and mixed together by the drone of the train.

I leaned my face against the cold window frame and started singing softly to pass the time, the anxiety, and the thumping of the wheels over metal tracks, which was making me carsick. My voice blended with the hums and clicks inside the train.

I was singing a song that was popular on the radio. Inside my head, I was pretending to be onstage with a microphone. I used to want to be a singer . . . before Ian told me I sing off-key. Now I kept my dreams to myself.

I stopped.

Ian had told me I sing off-key and here I was, and there was Ian. I lifted my face off the window and turned to look at him. Ian was watching me.

"Sorry," I said. "I forgot."

"For what?" Ian asked.

"I sing terrible and it bothers you," I reminded him.

The man behind the newspaper rustled his section. He turned the page over, snapped it into place, and was still again.

"If I tell you the truth about that, you won't get all nutsy on me, will you?" Ian asked.

I didn't want to swear or promise up and down, or anything that might appear "nutsy." I nodded my head in agreement, then shook my head, realizing it might have looked like I was saying, "Yes, I would be nutsy."

"Well, when we first moved to New Paltz, I was about seven or eight. You were maybe five or something. I didn't ever want to go to sleep. I fought with Dad every night."

Ian was still talking to me. I didn't know where to look. I watched my hands in my lap, then a stain on the floor by my feet.

"I made Dad sing to me and then I screamed at him that he wasn't singing the right song. The one she sang. I'd have these major tantrums and after a while he'd just rub my back, and he didn't try to sing anymore and I stopped asking. That's when he started telling us bedtime stories."

Ian wasn't looking at me anymore. He was seeing something else, I guess.

"So when you sing, it kind of pisses me off. I don't know why," Ian said.

I glanced over to the man behind the paper to see if he had heard the bad word; maybe he had, maybe he hadn't. He didn't move.

"You can sing," Ian told me. "It sounds nice. You have a nice voice, actually. You don't sing off-key at all. I wouldn't even know it was you when you're singing."

My heart soared, but quietly, so as not to appear nutsy. *I have a nice voice? Like my mother?*

After 125th Street the train slipped into darkness underground. The other passengers began shifting around with movement; some gathered their papers, or reached for their coats, or ended their cellular phone conversations. We were almost there.

Ian nudged me impatiently. The start of all the activity

on the train must have made him anxious, like the train was only going to slow down and everyone had to jump out.

"Get your backpack off the ground," he said sharply. "We'll be there in a minute."

I didn't argue; I obeyed. I had no idea what to do when we got off the train. The times we had taken the train before to visit our grandfather and Nana (when she was alive) we had been greeted at the platform by wide-open arms. Nana would wrap her arms around me, and I would be enveloped by her tiny body and the smell of her perfume that would stay with me long after she let go. No one would be waiting this time. No one even knew we were here. Except Paul, I guessed.

"Your return ticket is in your backpack, isn't it?" Ian snapped. "Get it, before we have to get off."

The train hissed loudly then jolted to a stop. There were lights inside the tunnel but it was still dim. Men and women burst out of the train as soon as the doors slid apart. Then the whole mob moved forward in one direction down the platform and up a long incline. Men dropped their newspapers into huge bins in the center aisle while others rummaged through and took them out. I saw the man we sat across from drop in his paper and hurry along without missing a beat.

Ian and I were swept into the singular forward motion. Each step took us up from the darkness, and when we entered the main lobby of the terminal, the room was grandly lit with crystal chandeliers. Marble walls and floors flashed with pink hues. The ceiling arched to the sky, a sky alive with stars and the magical men and beasts drawn between them. This was Grand Central Station. It was the first time I really saw it. Huge and hollow, filled with hundreds of people. But no one person here was looking for me, Gabby Weiss.

Each stone arch indicated what lay beyond it — LEXINGTON AVENUE, SUBWAY SHUTTLE, 42ND STREET, NORTH BALCONY, TRACKS 100–117. We spun around for a while, reading the arches that surrounded us, till Ian pointed.

"Let's just get out of here so I can get my bearings," Ian said. He started walking quickly toward one of the huge bowed openings, which led, hopefully, to the street we wanted. I had to quicken my steps to catch him. I could hardly keep up.

I had to reach out and take hold of Ian's sleeve. Ian didn't turn when he felt the tug of my pull on his shirt, but he slowed his pace.

I moved so near I could feel Ian deliberately lift his arm away slightly, and as usual he pulled his hand just out of reach.

Chapter 34

Ian stood for a moment in the street with me beside him. Outside we were immediately hit by the harsh sunshine and loud city noises. People were in even more of a hurry out here, and there were more of them, dodging in and out between the others, cutting ahead by jumping off the sidewalk and scooting faster to get in front of someone else. There was no time to stand still, no place to if you wanted.

"What's the address again?" Ian said. He had to shout.

"Four thirty-five East Seventy-ninth Street."

Ian and I both squinted up to see the street sign ahead, but neither of us could make it out.

"Let's start walking this way," I said, pointing. "And if the streets don't start going up, we'll know we should be walking the other way," I suggested. New York was no place to look lost.

Without a better plan, Ian agreed. We pushed our way to the end of the block and read the sign. Forty-first Street.

"Wrong way," Ian said. "Let's cut over the avenue

here." He stepped down off the curb when the light said WALK in white letters.

Ian had us cross over to 3rd Avenue and head east. We passed 41st, 42nd, 43rd, and 44th and things started to quiet down. The streets were wider and there were less people. I finally was able to unhunch my shoulders and relax the feeling of being potentially lost and swallowed up by the crowds.

"We'll walk to First Avenue and get a cab from there," Ian told me.

I was admiring Ian's confidence in finding the right direction as I followed beside him down the wide city blocks. Then, there was a river. Right in front of us. It was out of reach by at least two concrete sidewalks, a walkway, yellow barriers, and nothing less than a highway called the FDR, but there it was.

"Look." I pointed.

"So?" Ian looked.

"A river, here in New York City," I said as if I couldn't believe it. "I wonder if our mother walked here and saw this river."

I thought of myself and the steep walls of the Wallkill, the poison ivy growing along its banks, how I loved to watch the quiet water traveling by. Maybe this is why. Maybe I saw this river as a baby, with my mother.

"She didn't live anywhere near here," Ian said coldly. "We've got forty blocks to go. You really didn't think this through very well, did you?"

"Oh," I said.

We walked about midway up the block, then stopped.

"Why are we stopping?" I asked.

"We can't walk there and back and be back in time for the train. I'm getting us a taxi, remember?" Ian snapped. He was obviously losing patience with me. "You would have been completely lost," Ian said.

I wasn't going to follow him anymore.

"Do you want to do this?" I said. "'Cause you're acting really mean, like you don't want to. So . . . I don't think you should. You don't have to go any farther. I can go by myself."

Ian lowered his taxi-hailing arm. A few cars went by, a string of buses, and a lot of cabs before Ian answered me.

"You know, I do want to do this," Ian said, softening his voice. "I guess . . . I guess . . . I'm a little nervous about it."

I thought then, I thought for the very first time, *What if Ian has a list, too, a list of "things I need a mother for"? What if he has his own stash of Styrofoam marigold containers in his closet?* I supposed he did. Or something like that, something he never told me about.

Just then he spotted a cab on our side of the street and waved his hand at the driver. I opened the door of the cab and scooted over. Ian told the driver the address of where we wanted to go.

"Seventy-ninth Street," Ian said, leaning forward toward the Plexiglas divider and speaking clearly. "Between York and First."

"How did you know that?" I asked Ian. "Between York and First?"

"I don't know," he said.

The cab took off through the streets and the traffic. This part of New York was more residential. Here, children walked beside their mothers, people had dogs and bags of groceries. There were window boxes and flowers on the front stoops. There were trees. Just as I had imagined.

The numbers of the streets got higher. Sixty-first, Sixty-second, Sixty-third . . . We headed uptown. Ian was keeping his eye on the taxi meter, which was also getting higher. $5.30 . . . $5.60 . . . $5.90.

"You can let us off at Seventy-seventh — right here is fine." Ian leaned close to the divider as he spoke to the driver again.

"Whatever you say, kid." The driver swerved the taxi over to the curb to let us out. I was fishing inside my backpack for my money. I should have begun looking earlier, as the numbers of the streets got closer to 79th. I was frantic. I had barely unzipped the top when Ian brushed my efforts away.

"I got it," he said. Ian handed the driver a five and two ones from his front pocket. *He's taking care of me,* I thought, and we got out.

I wished that I could say, when I stepped out of the cab, that this felt like home. "This is my neighborhood," I might say. But it was as unfamiliar as could possibly be.

184

We had been let out at the corner, where a little grocery store stood. Fruit lay out on a shelf leaning right into the sidewalk. It was filled with all colors and shapes of things to eat. One big bucket of fresh flowers stood beside it on each side. Food hung from baskets hooked onto the awning above, peanuts and dried beans.

Did she shop here? I looked up at the street number. Seventy-eighth Street. Only a block from her apartment. Had I been here before?

"Well?" Ian paused on the sidewalk. "Let's go."

We turned the corner at 79th and kept walking until we were directly across from 435 East 79th Street. And we stopped. The entrance had a long green awning and printed on the awning just under the numbers was a name — The York.

So this building has a name. Everything should have a name, I thought. Her building was named The York. My mother's name was Arlene.

"Wouldn't it be wild if she just walked out right this instant?" I said as we stood safely on the opposite side of the street.

"Yeah, I guess that would be wild," Ian said. He didn't laugh, and I hadn't meant it to be funny.

A long time ago, well, maybe not so long ago, when I was around eight years old, I had this whole fantasy. She, my mother, was still alive somewhere. It was just that she couldn't handle things and she needed to get away, even from us, her own kids. So my dad arranged this whole thing. He arranged for her to appear to have died, but really she was just escaping. She was living somewhere else, *as* someone else. She needed a little break. Every mom deserves a break sometime.

So I had this fantasy and at some point I almost started believing it, every detail. I imagined what she did for a job while she was hiding out — she worked in a florist shop, putting together beautiful bouquets of flowers. She changed her name — she was Nicole Freedman. She grew her hair long and wore loose-fitting clothing. She lived in a sun-filled apartment above the florist shop. She slept on a pullout corduroy couch.

I imagined that she had even fooled her own parents. The funeral was a farce to throw everyone off, so they wouldn't come looking for her, so she could be free — all put together by my dad. For her. That's what she *needed* and he loved her that much. He was a hero.

But the best part of the whole story was that someday she was going to come back. Come back for me. She'd be there when I need her most, and that year I really needed her. I was in third grade. I was so lonely and everything was so sad. It was the year Beth Moore's mother wouldn't let me come to her house anymore.

I did a lot of waiting for her to return. If there was ever a right time, it was then. I needed her that year, real bad. But she didn't come and by the time I was nine, I vowed I would never wait for anyone again.

So when I said to my brother, "Wouldn't it be wild . . . ?" it wasn't so wild. It's just that I had stopped waiting and stopped believing and now here I was. And all I wanted was to know the truth.

Chapter 35

"Wait, I just want to look from here for a while," Ian said.

So we looked out across the wide street to the building named The York, and for a long while Ian didn't say anything. It was a very tall apartment building, maybe thirteen stories or so, and made of a whitish brick. Every other window had a metal balcony that didn't look big enough for anyone to stand on.

I quickly lost interest in just staring at the building; obviously nothing important was going to happen to me from there. I looked over to my brother. He stood still, eyes fixed on one spot. If I were to see anything or learn anything, it was going to have to come from him. I tried to see my brother very carefully, as if for the first time, as if he had some magic power; as if he were a portal to memory that I was going to miss if I wasn't attentive enough.

"Okay, ready?" Ian said. He was apparently done.

He wasn't yet offering any insights, so I nodded and we walked up to the corner to cross the street. Someone was standing in front of the building. There was a doorman, just as there had been that morning, and this one guarded the door. He was young, with a ponytail and a gray uniform. He paced back and forth and then disappeared inside the building.

"Ian," I said as we neared the entrance. "Is that the same doorman?"

Ian looked, considered the possibility, and then said firmly, "No, our guy was old."

"Well, this doorman's not just going to let us in."

A lady with a miniature dog came up the street before us and approached the building. The doorman stepped out in greeting and opened the large glass door for her.

"We have to tell him why we are here," I said.

"Like it's that simple," Ian said.

A little boy and his father walked out. The little boy wore a navy jacket and tie and carried a fancy, leather schoolbag.

"I'll just tell him the truth," I said. I didn't wait for Ian's approval. I walked steadily up to the man wearing the gray jacket with gold buttons and a ponytail.

"Excuse me," I said. "We used to live in this building, a long time ago. Would it be all right if we just looked around inside — I mean, just inside the lobby here."

Ian had come up behind me. We could see in through the glass doors. We could see the lobby, the two potted plants, the mail chute, the doorman's station, and the two elevators by the far wall.

The young doorman looked back inside, as if trying to figure out what we might want to see inside, or what we might do damage to if we were lying. It would be his responsibility if we did something wrong and he had been the one to let us in.

Why would anyone want to just innocently look at the lobby of a building they used to live in? But then again, why not?

"I don't know," the doorman said.

Ian and I were still, and waited like two small children.

"Just real quick," I said.

"Just right in the lobby?" Ian added.

"It's not allowed," the doorman told us.

"Please," I said.

There was a great pause right then. I don't know exactly how much time passed.

"Well, don't take long." The doorman moved aside, not quite giving permission, but allowing us in.

Ian and I both agreed, and we stepped inside the building.

The lobby was big for a New York apartment building, bigger than my grandparents' lobby. It had a fancy carpeted section where two brand-new upholstered chairs and a table stood empty. The floor by the elevators and the stairwell looked as if it had been newly tiled.

"Nothing looks familiar," Ian said and shook his head. "Nothing."

"You're not trying," I said to Ian. "Walk around a little."

Ian didn't say anything. He moved toward the mail

chute. He walked over the tiles and back to the carpet. He shrugged.

"Nothing." Ian dropped into one of the soft, deep chairs. I took the other one. My hands rested high on the arms of the chair, lifted like wings. So this was it? Chrome and glass, a poshly decorated New York apartment-building lobby was going to be the beginning and the end all in one? No, it couldn't!

My heart began pounding as soon as the possibility of an idea reached my lips; my eyes smarted with tears, though I didn't feel sad.

"We have to go in the elevator," I said suddenly. "We have to ride up and then ride down again and come out just like we did that day."

Ian leaned forward to see me past his chair. "What?"

"We have to," I said.

Ian glanced over to the doorman, who was letting someone into the building; an old man walking with a cane. I followed the man with my eyes as he made his way to the elevators. He pushed the UP button and stepped into the first elevator car, which had opened immediately.

"The doorman's not going to let us do that!" Ian said to me.

"Let's just do it so fast he doesn't notice," I whispered.

"They've got cameras in the elevators. Look." Ian gestured with a sideways shift of his eyes.

I could hear the blood from my heart racing through

my body, not letting me alone, not letting me rest. It was partly fear, partly anticipation, partly determination, partly warding off possible disappointment. No!

"We'll be back before he can do anything," I said and stood up. The doorman had stepped out to the sidewalk to help a woman out of her taxi. "We've got to do it. Now," I said.

"Okay, we'll try it."

Ian and I got up as if we were going to leave the building. Then we cut quickly around the carpet toward the hall, to the fully closed elevator doors. The UP button lit up when Ian touched it. Then even though I knew it wouldn't help, I kept pushing the UP button over and over.

"He's coming," Ian turned back. The woman from the taxi had several packages, which the doorman was struggling with as he neared the outside doors. He took hold of the handle and pulled it open. As he held the packages, the woman entered through the door and headed right toward us.

Desperately, I pushed the button once again. The bell dinged sweetly and the doors spread apart. Just as the doorman put down the woman's belongings inside the lobby, the elevator shut with Ian and me inside.

But the elevator was not moving. It was waiting for a command.

"I don't know what floor we lived on," Ian told me.

My heart thumped so loudly I thought I could hear it outside my body. I was equally sure I could hear the doorman's footsteps running toward the elevator.

"So where do we go?" I asked frantically.

"The top, the top one," Ian said. "We'll just go all the way up."

Ian leaned over and hit number 14 on the control panel. The pull of gravity moved through my body like a strong wave. It was quiet inside the elevator.

"Is this what we did?" I asked. I looked at the walls around me and the carpeted floor for anything to spark recognition.

"I guess," Ian said quietly.

The numbers lit up one by one as the elevator rose. I supposed the doorman could see us in the monitor by now. I peered up at the camera in the corner of the ceiling and quickly down. Maybe he was calling the police or maybe he was running up the stairs to catch us when we got to the top and arrest us.

"Do you remember anything yet?" I asked. My impatience must have slipped out.

"No," Ian snapped. "So why don't you quit bothering me?"

The bell sounded again, the doors slid open, and we were on the top floor. We were met with only silence, and I felt more alone than I had all day.

We would have only a moment here on this floor, then the elevator would shut again and we would be traveling down; the doors would open at the bottom and it would be all over. And if we were lucky the doorman would just ask us to leave. But I would have failed. I was about to lose everything all over again.

"I'm getting out here," I said, stepping out into the hall.

"What the . . . ?" Ian said. "Are you crazy? What are you doing?" He stepped out but held his foot in the path of the closing elevator doors. The heavy doors banged against his sneaker and automatically reopened.

"Does this look familiar? Is this it?" I heard my voice rising. "Were we here? Is this even the right building?"

"I don't know!" Ian shouted. The elevator banged again against his foot. This time Ian pulled away and the doors shut. The elevator left without us.

I felt terrible. The hall was empty and much darker than the lobby had been. It echoed with our voices. It smelled of carpet glue and fresh paint.

That's when I realized the whole building must have been renovated, and just recently, judging from the paint smell, the shiny tiles in the lobby, and the modern electronic equipment for the doorman's station. It couldn't seem familiar, because it wasn't familiar!

"It doesn't look like anything I remember. What can I say?" Ian said harshly.

We were too late. Our memories had been torn off with the old wallpaper that had hung here and the old carpet that had been replaced. They had been carried away like debris in a flooding river, too far out of reach. I had made a terrible mistake in coming here. Ian was really mad at me, yelling at me.

Then Ian started talking.

He wasn't angry at all, only deeply sad.

"We'd been awake for a while, I guess longer than we were used to being up alone. Finally we went into her room and tried to wake her up. We tried to shake her and we even used a light from the desk and shined it in her face," Ian began. "But it didn't work. I don't know why we came down here. Or why I didn't just call Dad."

"Call Dad?" I said. "Call him where?"

"At his new apartment. He had moved out. We lived here alone," Ian said slowly, as if he was remembering. But I didn't know, perhaps he had known all along. Our dad had moved out and that's when this happened. It all happened only three weeks after he left, Ian told me then.

"We got into the elevator to go down to tell the doorman. To tell him she wouldn't wake up. We came down to get help." Ian told me the story. His story. My story.

He pushed the elevator button on the wall.

"It was my fault," Ian said to me as we waited. "If I had gotten that doorman to listen to me. If I had tried harder. Afterward, I couldn't get that out of my head. I should have made him believe us. I should have gotten him to help."

"Ian, you were seven years old," I told him, but I knew he knew that.

The bell sounded and the elevator doors opened again. We stepped inside. I didn't even think about the camera or the doorman. Ian and I stood side by side, facing out as the doors closed on us for a second time that day.

"I bet you were mad at me," I said. "I bet you didn't even want to take me with you."

"No, I wasn't," Ian said. "I wanted to take you with me. We were together. I think I was holding your hand."

Ian let his arm drop and his fingers unwind. I moved an immeasurable step closer to my brother and felt his hand reach out for mine. Our fingers encircled each other's as the elevator dropped past each floor. As soon as the door opened up to the natural light of the lobby the doorman came rushing over, red in the face, most definitely angry, and told us to leave the building at once or he was going to call the police. Ian and I didn't say anything. We didn't let go of each other. We were still gripping hands as we left The York and stepped out into the street.

Chapter 36

I can't say exactly where I left my backpack after that point. I didn't remember having it in the elevator; I sort of remembered having it while Ian and I sat on those big chairs in the lobby. I was sure I took it off the train with me. But after that I wasn't sure. All I was sure of was that I had my return ticket in the front zipper pocket, and Ian only had six dollars left in his wallet.

What I couldn't believe was that Ian didn't tell me how stupid I was or how careless or ask why had he gone on this idiotic expedition in the first place.

"I'll think of something," Ian said.

My face was pale, I'm sure. I felt like something had hold of my guts and was twisting them around. My mouth tasted like I had been chewing an eraser. I couldn't slow down my breathing and at the same time I couldn't get enough air. I had lost my ticket and my only way home. We couldn't call Dad. He would be angry beyond words. We didn't have enough for another ticket home. Paul was supposed to pick us up at the Poughkeepsie train station at five past three, but there was no way to reach him before then. He had band rehearsal — who knows where?

"We'll just start walking back to Grand Central Station," Ian said calmly.

"Then what?" My voice was thick, with sobs waiting in the back of my throat.

"We'll think while we're walking," Ian said. "But at least we'll be walking."

It seemed to make sense, and besides, he wasn't yelling. He didn't walk away and leave me, though he had one ticket to go home — his own. He wouldn't do that, anyway. He was my big brother.

We started away from the door, away from The York, away from her neighborhood.

"I'm so sorry," I said, and as soon as I spoke I began to cry. Tears didn't drop from my eyes gently onto my cheeks; tears poured like a river. I hadn't cried like this since Cleo left. And now I cried again. I cried for me.

"It's all my fault," I kept saying, and we kept on walking. Every now and then someone, usually a woman with children, would ask if I was all right; to which my brother would have to answer, "She's okay. I'm her brother."

It was as if everything I had ever done wrong, and every time I had ever been lonely, and every time I had ever felt that I never would and never could be as good as everyone else hit me all at once. Had I never asked Cleo if I could call her "Mom" she never would have left. Had I been quieter in the mornings my real mother would be alive. If I was more deserving she would have left the florist shop and come back for me. I had needed her so badly. I needed her now.

The neighborhood around us changed the more we headed downtown on Lexington Avenue. It got busier and more crowded. My crying slowed, but my lungs involuntarily gasped for air every few seconds.

"Then it's my fault, too," Ian said quietly. We waited at a curb for the light to change. People behind us stepped up and waited. People on the other side facing us waited.

"I shouldn't have let you hold your ticket," Ian continued. "Or I should have been wearing the backpack. I'm older."

"But this whole thing was my idea," I said. The light turned to WALK and the mobs headed forward directly into each other, but somehow all the people in that little space avoided bumping, crossed the street, and continued on their opposite ways.

"I wanted to go, too," Ian said. "I told you that already. What? You don't hear so well?" He knocked me on the top of my head with his fist, lightly.

"Well, then Dad's really the one to blame," I said.

"For you losing your ticket?"

"No, it's his fault that she died," I said. "He moved out and then she died."

The tall buildings surrounded us here. Department stores and banks, and hundreds of people rushing again. The sidewalk was narrow. There were no trees. There was barely sky. Shade on one side of the street, sun on the other, and in between a flood of traffic moving in one direction like a river.

"Then it's really her fault, isn't it?" Ian said. "Because she didn't *die* — she killed herself."

It was the first time he had said that; the first time I had heard that — And I knew it was true. *She* had killed herself. Not me. It was not my responsibility to keep my mother alive. She had not taken too many sleeping pills because I was too noisy in the morning. Ian could not have saved her by convincing the doorman. If it hadn't been that time, she would have found another time.

But I had come back to the last place and the last time I'd had a mother, and by doing so I acknowledged and even embraced her existence.

And I said good-bye.

Chapter 37

We were mostly quiet the rest of the way, and so when we got to Grand Central we still had no plan. I remembered that Taylor was staying with her dad in New York City. Ian bought a pack of gum at a newsstand to get change for the pay phone. Now we had five dollars left. I called information and asked for Such. S-u-c-h. Fortunately there was only one in Manhattan. I dialed the number I was given by a recording.

"Oh, Gabby," Taylor answered anxiously. "Where are you?"

"What do you mean?" I was confused by her worry. As far as she should know, I was simply calling her from my home in New Paltz.

"Your father, Gabby," Taylor explained. "He's been looking all over for you. The flooding from the Wallkill knocked out the power at the university. All the weekend classes were canceled and your dad's been home all morning. All afternoon . . . gee, it's three-thirty already. He's really worried, Gabby."

"He called you?" I was too shocked to figure this out. "In New York?"

At this point Ian realized the point of the conversation.

"Dad called?" Ian mouthed to me. "Where?"

The first thing I felt was scared. Dad was going to be mad, really mad, maybe madder than he's ever been at us before. But I was mad, too, and he had a lot of talking to do when I got home.

"Gabby, are you there?" It was Taylor.

"I'm here. I'm in New York City."

"Gabby, what are you doing in New York? Even though, I think I have a pretty good idea," Taylor said.

"We were looking for something I'd lost," I told Taylor.

"Did you find it?"

I looked over at Ian. I felt the power of what we had just done. Maybe what we had been looking for wasn't exactly what we found. Nothing had happened. And yet everything had happened.

"Yeah," I said. "We did."

"Good . . . Oh, wait, my dad wants to talk to you," Taylor said abruptly.

The phone was in my hands pressing against my ear. I listened.

"Gabby?" the new voice said. "This is Taylor's dad, Walter Such. Where are you kids?"

He sounded kind. Not mad. I suddenly wanted someone to just pick us up and take us home. I wanted so badly to go home.

"We're at Grand Central Station," I told the voice.

"Stay right there. I'll be over in a cab to get you. Stand at the corner of Forty-second and Lexington. On the side of the station. And wait. I'll find you," he ordered.

That's exactly what we did and about fifteen minutes later a yellow taxi pulled up with Taylor inside waving frantically. Beside her, peering forward to see us, was an older man with a graying beard in dark clothes. He appeared a round figure, more friendly and welcoming than I had anticipated. The cab door swung open.

"Gabby? Ian? Get in. I'm Walter Such. It's okay, we called your father already," the man said. "We let him know you were safe."

It was a short trip to Taylor's father's apartment. I saw that Taylor and her dad kept one hand on each other at all times. She wasn't afraid to touch him. And he always hugged her back. And so I saw that it was from her father that Taylor got her kindness and her generous touch.

Ian and I didn't say a word; not to each other nor to anyone else. Taylor did all the talking.

"First, your dad called my mom, but she was out with Richard and I don't know where. I think he called Ian's friend, remember, the one you thought was cute. What's his name? Oh, whatever. But he wasn't home, either. Anyway, he finally got my mom and she said I was in New York this weekend. I don't know why your dad thought to call here, but . . . I've been worried about you all day, too. . . ."

We arrived at the address and the driver pulled over. It

was still light out when we got out of the cab, though the sun was low between two buildings and reached out with long, yellow fingers, as if pointing directly at us.

Finally, Ian spoke. "Why are we coming here?"

We all walked up the few steps to the apartment, following Taylor's father.

"I mean, wouldn't it have been easier to just lend us the train fare?" Ian continued.

Mr. Such turned the key in the first door, which led to a small vestibule inside and another locked door. "Your dad wants to come here and pick you up. He was really worried about you, Ian. I don't think you understand."

"Yeah, right," Ian mumbled. "He's real worried."

I was too afraid to speak. I no longer had the desire to confront my father. I was too tired and by now fiercely thirsty. I was probably hungry, too, but I couldn't feel it. My legs ached. I could feel a huge blister on my left heel.

We walked through the second door and to Mr. Such's apartment. It was on the ground floor. Another key opened the inner door. It was all so odd and different, being here and wanting to be here but knowing I wasn't supposed to be here.

Taylor, Ian, and I watched TV while we waited for my dad to arrive. Mr. Such offered us something to eat, but Ian wouldn't have anything. I wanted only a drink, please.

Taylor cornered me when I went to put my glass in the sink.

"I knew it. I knew it about you the first time I met you, up on the hill. Remember, Gabby?" Taylor said.

I could hardly muster the strength to respond. "What are you talking about?" I asked.

"You did it, Gabby." Taylor took my arm. "You were scared but you did it. You went to New York. You looked for your mother. I always knew you were brave."

"Me?"

"I think your mother would be so proud of you," Taylor said.

I think maybe Taylor was right.

When the doorbell rang in the three tones we all jumped. Mr. Such got up to answer it. When my dad walked in I thought I had never seen how old he was before. He was slightly bent, his hair was mussed, his face was drawn with deep lines around his eyes and his mouth. He looked as though he had worn his worry all day.

Ian and I were expecting the teeth gritting, huffing, angry face that we have witnessed before. I had seen it when I accidentally turned on the lawn mower and it ran through my dad's tomato plants. And I think Ian had seen that particular face of our dad's even more than I had.

Our dad had driven all the way in from New Paltz to get us, we had been missing all day, he had to call strange people and parents he didn't know, looking for his two children. I would be mad, if it were me.

And yet there he stood, worn-out and sad. I knew then that Taylor, who always talks too much when she gets nervous, had told my dad why we came to New York. He knew what we had been looking for and where we had gone.

"I was so scared," he said. He lifted his arms. "I don't know what I'd do if . . ." He didn't finish his sentence.

He wasn't angry at all. He sounded sad and worried and nearly as lonely as could be. I wanted only to be held by those arms that were reaching for me. When I got inside, right up close next to his body, I could feel my dad's arms still open. For Ian.

I buried my face into my dad's shirt, into the familiar warmth that was my father. He smelled of oil paints and turpentine. Ian took his time. I could hear his feet shuffle slowly across the wood floor. When he was close enough, he stopped. My dad ruffled Ian's hair and let him go, but Ian stood close by. Then my father closed his arms around me tightly. I could have stayed that way for a long, long time.

Chapter 38

We all went to dinner, Taylor and her father and Ian, me, and our dad. Walter Such knew some great Mexican restaurant in the Village. It turned out to be one of the most wonderful, fun nights of my whole life. Walter Such was an artist, too. Not a painter like my dad, but a photographer. He said he worked "as mild-mannered ad-agency guy by day and by night as the mad shutter-bug man." That was his joke. He and Ian and my dad got along really well. They talked about "art."

Nobody talked about what happened or what Ian and I did, or why. Still no one said her name. No one mentioned 435 East 79th Street. But we would soon, I knew. We had a lot to talk about.

Taylor kept nudging me all through dinner and making faces. Finally she said she had to go to the bathroom and did I want to go?

"No, I don't have to," I said.

"But, really, you *should*." Taylor lifted her face in that funny way that only a YBF can see.

I finally got the message she was transmitting with her

eyebrows. I agreed to accompany Taylor to the bathroom, even though I really didn't have to go.

"So what is it already?" I asked Taylor. We stood inside the tiny bathroom with a naked bulb and the metal pull-chain dangling just above our heads. The bathroom was only meant for one person and probably a tiny person at that.

"I got it," Taylor whispered, though I could pretty well say for certain that we were alone. "I could hardly wait to tell you."

I smiled. "You got your period?"

"Yeah. Yesterday, when I got to my dad's." Taylor nodded her head up and down. "My dad didn't know what to do. He was so nervous. I'm so glad you already told me everything I needed to know," Taylor said.

Funny, wasn't it? After all, it was from me that Taylor had gotten her information. It was me, Gabby Weiss, girl without mother, who gave out advice on womanhood to my best friend, Taylor Such. Imagine that!

Taylor was going on and on. "And Gabby, I'm so glad you're my best friend. I'm so happy you're here tonight, even if it had to happen like it did. . . . I was . . . Oh my God, watch out for the toilet!"

In my excitement for Taylor's news I had stepped back a little and was now practically falling into the toilet, which was open, and had no lid even if someone had wanted to close it.

"Watch out for the toilet?" I laughed. It sounded so funny.

"Yeah, watch out for the toilet," Taylor repeated, catching on right away, because we were YBFs.

I said, "I looove the chocolate glaze."

"Got milk?" Taylor answered.

"Hurry, get a paper towel," I added my line.

"Why be elves!?" Taylor said.

"Watch out for the toilet," I finished the sequence to date.

When someone started banging on the door and shouting to us in Spanish we doubled over and laughed so hard. We hugged and laughed and nearly *did* fall in the toilet. And when we unlatched the door and spilled out, we both had stupid, laughing faces, watery eyes, and blotchy red cheeks.

Chapter 39

My Journal
The red book - last entry

You'll never believe, or rather <u>I'll</u> never believe, when
I read this twenty years from now, because
that's how long I'm going to wait till I open this
journal again and read it. This will be my last entry, since there are only a few pages left and
then I'll have to start a new one. This is the red
book that Cleo gave me almost a whole year ago.
Every time I pick it up I remember how awful I
felt when I realized Cleo was gone, and then when
I saw the inscription page torn out (you can still
see the ripped part in the front of the book), you
can imagine.

I used to pretend I didn't care about Cleo. I
was afraid, I guess. Being afraid can stop you
from doing a lot of things. It can stop you from
wanting to know the truth. It can stop you from
telling someone you love them. I'm trying to teach
my dad not to be so afraid but he's a slow learner.

My mother was afraid, too. I've come to understand, sort of, why she did what she did. She was

afraid when she and my dad broke up and she didn't think she could go on. I think what she really wanted was for my dad to come over and find her and save her. I don't think she really wanted to die. But it didn't happen like that. I'm still sad sometimes, and sometimes I feel lonely again. But I'll never be that afraid, no matter how bad things get.

I don't know if I'll ever find out what really happened. I've talked to Grandpa, and Ian some more, and Dad, and even some old friends of my mother's that my dad told me about. Everyone has their own story. Now, I have mine.

Cleo did come back (she's been back for a while now) but that's not what I was going to say. I was going to say: You'll never believe what I found! The other barrette!

I was riding my bicycle home from school (seventh grade is really hard, by the way), and just as I turned down my dirt-road driveway I saw it. Right in the middle of the road. It wasn't even muddy or dirty. I still have the first one Taylor and I found. It's safe in the drawer of my night table, but I've never worn it.

Now I've got them both back. It's like a miracle because I don't know how long it's been there, or how many times I just went right by it without noticing, or how it got there in the first place. And stayed in perfect condition!

A miracle.

Which reminds me, Dad told me it was my mother who named me Gabby (he's been trying to tell me little things as they come up and Cleo is helping to make him do it). Gabby is short for Gabrielle (I already knew that part) and Gabrielle is the girl version of Gabriel, who was an angel. An archangel. They _were_ going to name me Zoe, but when my mother first saw me after I was born, she said I was truly an angel, her angel, and she named me Gabrielle. I've started signing my papers in school like that. Gabrielle Weiss.

Which reminds me again, Taylor and I have George, but for earth science this time. He said last year's flood was the worst New Paltz has seen in a hundred years - more sediment was dumped on the flood plain than modern farmers have had the pleasure of enjoying in a long while (he said that!). He said that when a river floods it deposits nutrients all over the ground, which is why crops grow so well here. I believe Mr. Everett about the river and the flooding water. But not for the reasons he talks about. The river brought me my two barrettes again, and pretty soon I'm going to get up the courage to wear my hair down with two butterflies alighting for a brief rest.

So, Cleo _is_ back with my dad again. My dad went all the way to Colorado on a plane shortly after our adventures in New York City just to ask Cleo to come back. And she did. They aren't married yet.

212

Soon maybe, but Cleo, she keeps telling me how sorry she is that she hurt me by tearing that page out when she left. She said sometimes grown-ups make really big mistakes that they can't even make up a good excuse for. I suppose I can relate to that.

I'm still deciding if I can totally forgive Cleo or not. But I've got time for all that.

I'm only thirteen.